MW00933465

Autumn in Your Arms

A novel by

Sherene Funk

Autumn in Your Arms Copyright 2016 by Sherene Funk.

All rights reserved. This book or any portion thereof may not be reproduced or used in any manner whatsoever without the express written permission of the author.

This is a work of fiction. All of the characters, organizations, and events portrayed in this novel are either products of the author's imagination or are represented fictitiously.

ISBN-13: 9781523205851
ISBN-10: 1523205857

Dedication

For my husband, Keith,
my true love and best friend.

Acknowledgments

Many thanks to Deanne Blackhurst, Devin Giovaere, and Amy Harke-Moore for their invaluable editorial insights. I'd also like to give a shout out to the CreateSpace team for helping me achieve my personal goal of publishing a book.

1

"Earth to Rina!"

Marina Thatcher blinked as if shaking off the remnants of a spell. "Sorry, Erik. I don't know why I'm so distracted tonight," she lied, grateful when her coworker and best friend swung her away from the cause of her preoccupation.

Not for the first time that evening, she'd found her gaze wandering to the compelling figure standing near the periphery of the dance floor. The man's chiseled features were certainly worthy of a fairytale prince, but Foster Delaney was hardly a fantasy she could afford to indulge in, even for one night.

It was kind of hard not to when the atmosphere hummed with magic. Marina marveled at how the event planning company hired to decorate the summer kick-off party for Argyle Media Solutions had transformed the hotel ballroom.

The leafy canopy overhead was illuminated by thousands of twinkling fairy lights. The tables, scattered among lifelike trees and lush foliage, were draped in iridescent fabric that sparkled in the amber candlelight flickering within rustic lantern centerpieces. In such a setting, it was easy to imagine she'd been transported from Portland, Maine, to an enchanted forest in some far off land.

Marina tried to shake off the ethereal effects of the décor. At twenty-eight, she was too old to be entertaining fanciful notions of enchanted forests, let alone romantic thoughts of her employer.

"Why aren't you dancing with your fiancée?" she asked her dance partner.

"She told me to dance with you." Erik shrugged.

"Oh, thank you." Marina let out an indignant snort. "I'm so flattered."

"No offense, Rina," Erik smirked. "But dancing is a lot more fun with a woman who finds me irresistibly attractive and can't keep her hands off me."

"Then maybe you should dance with Deidra Torres."

"She doesn't waste her time on small fish like me." He snickered derisively. "Of course, that doesn't mean she wouldn't smash my gills on her way to hooking a bigger catch."

Marina lifted her shoulders in a dismissive shrug. Who Deidra sank her hooks into was none of her business. Besides, her attention was immediately riveted elsewhere when Erik led her into a turn that restored her view of Delaney.

Her pulse escalated as her eyes once again drank in the sight of her employer. It wasn't that she was unaccustomed to seeing Foster Delaney all decked out in a fancy suit. But for some reason, the fitted gray ensemble he wore tonight perfectly accentuated the svelte lines of his athletic body. His short brown hair was stylishly mussed, and the jewel-toned silk shirt he wore intensified his green gaze. Had his eyes always been the color of Irish moss?

A shiver of awareness skittered along her nerves as she realized that those very eyes were staring right back at her. She hastily dipped her head, embarrassed that Delaney had caught her watching him.

"What's wrong?"

Marina looked up to find Erik studying her with narrowed eyes. "Nothing." She tried to shrug it off, even as she felt her cheeks warming.

Erik glanced in the direction that had riveted her attention and then turned back to her with a questioning brow.

"Like I said," she replied with a smile that she hoped was convincing, "it's nothing."

Moments later, when the music stopped, Erik was the one smiling as he deftly spun Marina directly into Foster Delaney's path.

"Take her off my hands, will you?" Erik clapped Delaney on the shoulder and hurried away from them, leaving Marina too stunned to speak. But that didn't stop her from leveling a murderous scowl at his retreating back.

Delaney swung her into the cradle of his arms, and she couldn't help the shiver of anticipation that ran through her as his hand pressed against the small of her back. His eyes flared slightly, as if surprised at how his touch had affected her, but his facial expression gave nothing away and his tone of voice was perfectly normal when he spoke.

"You look lovely tonight."

"Thank you." She dropped her gaze, forcing herself to focus on something other than the strong, muscular column of his throat and the way his hard muscles felt beneath her hand. She'd have to work harder at schooling her emotions if she wished to keep the carefully constructed walls around her heart from crumbling.

Marina silently cursed the party's fairytale atmosphere for messing with her head so thoroughly. Lifting her gaze to a point beyond Delaney's shoulder, she concentrated on picking out her friends among the crowd. Suki Bennett, the only woman at Argyle she considered a true friend, was chatting with Erik and his fiancée, Jill Calahan. But where was Suki's date?

Marina frowned when she spotted Milo Drescher engaged in conversation with Deidra Torres near an exit door. His stance was stiff, hands fisted at his sides. Deidra's arms were folded beneath her ample chest, her posture oozing the predatory confidence of a large cat ready to pounce upon its helpless victim. Marina lost sight of them momentarily as Delaney guided her through the turns of the dance. When they came into view again, Deidra leaned in close and said something that made Milo flinch back. With a come-hither crook of her finger, she slipped out of the ballroom. Milo jammed his hands into his pockets and followed Deidra, but Marina didn't miss the lingering glance he cast Suki as he stalked from the room.

Following the direction of his gaze, Marina studied the petite Asian woman sitting with her other friends. If Suki had any concerns about Milo, it certainly didn't show. In fact, the serene look on her face suggested that all was right with her world. Marina sincerely hoped that it was. Their relationship was so new, having blossomed several weeks earlier with some prompting from Erik.

"I heard about your dog attack last month."

Marina startled back to the present at the sound of Delaney's voice. Groaning inwardly, she wondered why Erik had felt the need to share that particular detail with her employer. "Yes, well, fortunately Erik was there to pry the little devil off my ankle."

"There were no residual physical damages, I hope?"

"All my limbs are functioning at optimum levels," she confirmed offhandedly.

"Good to know." He chuckled. For a moment he said nothing, then there was a palpable shift in the tone of his voice. "So, aside from random dog attacks, how has *everything else* been?"

Marina tensed. Even though he hadn't actually said the words, she suspected Delaney was referring to that day in February, nearly four months ago, when she'd fled the office building on the verge of a total meltdown. Her sister, Tasha, had been gone almost a month by then, but Marina was having a particularly miserable day.

After careening blindly across the street, she'd stumbled through the park to collapse upon a wooden bench dusted in frost. Inhaling the icy air deep into her lungs, she'd willed it to numb the raw hurt inside.

How much time had passed, Marina couldn't say. But she became aware that she was no longer shivering. Shifting her gaze, she noticed that a thick wool coat had been draped around her shoulders, and Delaney's warm body sat next to her on the bench. He never said a word, hadn't bothered trying to tell her everything was going to be OK. He'd simply sat beside her.

At some point, he'd stood to leave. "I've got to get back. Why don't you take the rest of the day off?" he suggested, squeezing her shoulder.

"I'm OK now." She shook her head, rising from the bench. "I'll walk back with you."

"Marina..." There was a thick quality to his voice, the gentleness of his tone unmistakable. "You don't have to. Whatever you have on your plate can wait until tomorrow or the next day...Whenever you're ready to come back."

"I appreciate that," she'd said. "But I *need* to work."

His eyes, a misty gray-green underneath the leaden sky, studied her face for a long moment. The concern she saw in his expression caused her heart to lurch with a longing she'd never experienced before. She wanted him to crush her against his chest, to feel his breath warm against her ear as he whispered tender words meant only for her.

The intensity of her feelings in that moment had surprised and frightened her, and it had taken the sheer force of her will to keep them contained. Later, though, Marina had convinced herself that her reaction to Delaney that day had more to do with the thoughtfulness he'd extended to her in a moment of vulnerability than any true affection she might have felt for him.

The memory receded into the background, and the ballroom came back into focus again as Delaney whispered, "You know I'm always here for you, right?"

"Yes," Marina answered on a wistful sigh. If only the song they were dancing to would end so she could quell the disorienting emotions fluttering through her body. But apparently the DJ had chosen the longest ballad known to mankind, giving Delaney plenty of time to make more awkward inquiries.

"Erik mentioned that you and Grayson split up?" he asked solicitously. "It must have been hard to deal with that on top of everything else."

"Oh, uh..." Marina grimaced.

"Forget it," he interrupted, shaking his head. "I shouldn't have brought it up."

"It's all right." She wished Erik hadn't shared the news of her failed relationship with her employer. But it wasn't Delaney's fault, and now that he knew about it, there was no sense being evasive. "It was for the best," she shrugged.

"Still, I'm sorry."

It was probably just her imagination, but something about the way he said it—as if he weren't sorry at all, as if he were *relieved* she was no longer tied to another man—made her glance up. Their gazes locked, the air crackling between them like currents of electricity. Delaney's eyes narrowed, and his mouth opened wordlessly. He leaned away from her, putting more distance between them.

"Sir, it's time for your speech." The male voice came from just behind Marina.

Delaney's arms dropped away from her body. With an abrupt nod, he turned and strode toward the front of the ballroom.

Stunned, Marina wandered off the dance floor in a daze. What had just passed between them? Whatever it was, it felt as real as what she'd experienced in the park that day in February, only more frightening.

She tried to convince herself that any attraction she felt for Delaney tonight was purely chemical, a condition brought on by the romantic atmosphere. Come Monday morning, when the spell of the evening had long worn off, it would be easier to view him as nothing more than her employer.

Marina took further comfort in the knowledge that, on the off chance her feelings for Delaney hadn't snapped back to their familiar professional confines by then, he would be leaving on a series of business trips the following month.

She wouldn't see him for weeks at a time over the course of the summer. Surely his prolonged absences would cool the feelings of ardor he'd awakened in her tonight?

— ﹏

As summer faded into fall, Marina was pretty sure she had a bigger problem than the one she'd faced at the summer kickoff party back in May.

She could no longer deny that her fondness for Delaney had grown more intense during his absences.

Of all the men she could be interested in, why did it have to be the CEO of Argyle Media Solutions? If his social status as one of *Forbes'* top-ten business leaders in the world didn't make him completely unattainable to her, his position as her employer most certainly did.

What was more, past experience had taught Marina to be wary of her own emotions when it came to a handsome face. Hadn't Tasha warned her repeatedly not to fall too hard, too fast, for the gorgeous Grayson Munro?

But it was more than physical attraction she felt for Delaney. In fact, since the night she'd danced with him, she'd felt a fundamental shift in her affection for him. When he was away on his many business trips, she'd discovered that she sincerely missed their discussions, work related or otherwise. And at night, as she lay in bed, she'd found herself wondering what Delaney was doing. But she'd abandoned that practice when thoughts of him spending time in the company of other women had caused a painful squeeze in her chest.

Marina sensed intuitively that Delaney was a different sort of man than Grayson. She knew he wouldn't have walked out on her during one of the lowest points in her life, as Grayson had. In fact, she hadn't seen or heard from him in nearly eight months.

So why had Grayson started calling her again out of the blue? Well, it hardly mattered. She had no intention of giving her ex the time of day. Besides, she was too busy trying to suppress her growing affection for her employer.

Marina pushed thoughts of Grayson and Delaney aside to admire the scene beyond the floor-to-ceiling windows of her office. The waning pinks and oranges of an October sunrise had given way to a cloud-strewn blue sky, and the trees lining the streets below were bright beacons crowned in burning shades of orange, red, and yellow.

With a sigh, she turned back to the dwindling stack of files in front of her. Was it only Wednesday? With all the extra time she was spending at the office, the days and weeks seemed to blur together. She'd made a huge dent in her workload, somehow managing to put off Erik's frequent attempts to lure her away from the office for coffee breaks, leisurely walks through in the park during lunch, and early weekday dinners with him and his fiancée. Still, she appreciated his efforts.

In the absence of parental support, she didn't know how she'd have survived these past ten months without the ostensibly arrogant, superstitious, lovable tease of a man whom she was fortunate enough to have as a co-worker and dear friend.

A shiver suddenly snaked up Marina's spine.

Her head snapped up to find Foster Delaney staring at her through the glass-paneled front wall of her office. Immediately her mind flashed back several months to the first time he'd returned from one of several long business trips he'd taken over the summer. She'd caught him brooding at her then, too. Come to think of it, he'd eyed her with the same contemplative expression each time he'd returned from another trip.

Delaney stiffened when her gaze collided with his, a tight grimace pulling at one corner of his mouth as if something pained him. With a curt nod, he stalked down the hall.

Pulse racing, Marina sagged against the back of her chair and slowly expelled the breath she hadn't realized she was holding.

What the devil was that about?

2

Marina was still puzzling over her employer's brooding stare when he summoned her to his office late that afternoon. Stopping just outside his suite, she inspected her reflection in the huge hall mirror. Glacier blue eyes stared back at her, narrowing in dissatisfaction as she smoothed an imaginary wrinkle in her gray sheath dress and tucked a stray lock of onyx colored hair back into the chignon at the nape of her neck. Leaning closer, she dabbed at her lips, wishing she'd applied a bit of gloss to amplify their delicate shape.

She frowned at her reflection, at the telltale flush of pink staining her cheeks. No matter how hard she tried to smother it, every time she thought of seeing Delaney these days, her stomach fluttered and her heart thudded as though he were her first high school crush. *But he isn't,* she sternly reminded herself. *He's your boss, and he hardly asked you here for a social call.*

Normally, Marina could guess exactly what Foster Delaney wanted to discuss. After finally managing to secure the long-awaited Hiroshi InnovaTech deal, the client had started living up to the company's fastidious reputation. Recently, she and Delaney had discussed, at length, how they might keep Hiroshi from derailing all the work they'd invested in the company's advertising and social media campaigns. And on Monday, they'd had a very productive conference call with Hiroshi. Surely everything they'd accomplished during that meeting hadn't started to unravel already?

As much as Marina didn't want to consider such a possibility, she couldn't come up with another good reason why her employer would ask to see her so late in the afternoon on a day he typically reserved for meetings with VIP clients.

Unless...

Marina caught her bottom lip between her teeth, recalling her after-hours encounter with Foster Delaney the previous Friday evening. Squinting in concentration, she replayed the memory of that night through her mind.

— ⌣ —

Erik and his fiancée, Jill, had insisted on taking Marina out for dinner at their favorite Irish pub. The turn-of-the-century building boasted reclaimed brick walls and photos dedicated to Portland's immigrant history. A fire crackled cheerfully in the nearby stone hearth as live acoustic music floated through the crowded room, competing with the steady hum of conversation. The lively atmosphere wrapped around Marina, boosting her spirits.

Until the last person she expected to see sauntered through the door and shattered her composure.

"Hey, there's Delaney," Erik announced and waved him over to their booth.

Marina shot her friend a warning glare, but it was too late. Her employer was already moving toward them with long, purposeful strides.

Watching him stole the breath from her chest. At nearly six feet, he wasn't as tall or broad as Erik, but his bearing was one of innate confidence, his movements effortless and graceful. The dance she'd shared with him at the company's summer kickoff party in May had more than hinted at his athletic form, at a chest that was hard and sculpted and arms that were strong and muscular. Marina ducked her head, hoping Delaney wouldn't notice the flush spreading over her face.

Not taking his eyes off her, Delaney addressed the small group. "Mind if I join you?"

"Please." Erik gestured to the empty booth space next to Marina, which inspired her to give her friend's shin a hard kick under the table.

"Thanks for letting me share your table," Delaney said after a waiter had taken his order for a Coke and sandwich.

"No problem." Erik slid his arm around his fiancée. "Marina spotted you and suggested we invite you over."

Marina kicked him harder that time and was rewarded with a satisfying grunt. She cast a quick glance at Delaney and immediately wished she hadn't. His green gaze, luminous under the hanging table lamp, shimmered over her and made her insides tremble.

She spoke little during the meal and mostly picked at her food while Delaney and Erik debated everything from football to politics. Jill rolled her eyes at them and launched into a discussion on potential wedding venues.

Almost before Delaney could stuff the last bite of sandwich in his mouth, Erik dragged him toward the game area to flaunt his dart-throwing skills. Marina blew out a sigh, grateful for the respite. Maybe now her breathing would return to normal.

Jill wasted no time making her point as soon as the two men had slid out of the booth. "He's hot!"

Marina smiled indulgently at her friend. "He's my boss, Jill."

"Does it matter?"

"It does to me," Marina replied, in all seriousness. But she had to bite back the urge to laugh as Jill frankly perused her employer's denim-clad backside.

"Oh come on, Rina," Jill shot back. "You need to live a little. And while we're on the subject of living"—she eyed Marina disapprovingly, pursing her lips for effect—"do you even own a pair of jeans?"

"You sound like Tasha." Marina rolled her eyes, but she was smiling inside. It pleased her that Jill had recently started calling her *Rina*. Somehow, it made her feel closer to the woman who was going to marry her best friend. "What's wrong with what I'm wearing?" she inquired, gesturing at her respectable silk blouse and fitted, gray trousers.

"Nothing, I guess. But—" Jill cut her sentence short, lifting her hand to her mouth as if she were about to be sick.

"Are you all right?"

"Sorry," she apologized when the moment had passed. "I don't know if it was my dinner or the way this place smells tonight, but something apparently doesn't agree with me."

"Do you need to go home?" Marina asked with concern. "Should I get Erik?"

"No, no." Jill waved it off. "What I was trying to say is you have a great butt for jeans, and it's totally being wasted on business casual wear. But never mind your clothes—" She wiggled her eyebrows, her lovely hazel eyes alight with an impish twinkle. "I want to talk about *you* engaging in a torrid office romance with *that!*" She pointed a long, manicured finger at Delaney's backside.

"Would you please stop?" Marina groaned.

Jill sobered, glancing between Marina and the men at the dartboard, where Erik was frowning at Delaney's steady hand and near-perfect aim. "It's just that...well, ever since Tasha's death, and then that ugly business with Grayson..." She paused. "We just want you to be happy."

"I know." Marina gave her hand a squeeze. "Thank you for worrying about me. But I'm fine, really."

"OK." Jill nodded, settling back against her seat. "Uh-oh." She pointed at the two men walking toward them, weaving around the tables of the crowded pub. "Erik does *not* look amused. Your Mr. Delaney must have whipped him good."

"He's not *my* Mr. Delaney!" Marina said, emphasizing each word in hushed tones as the men approached the table. Pulling Erik aside, she whispered her concern in his ear.

Erik's brows furrowed. Crossing to Jill's side, he slipped a hand around her shoulder. "Marina say's you're not feeling so hot. Why don't you stay here while I go pull the car around, hmm?"

Jill's gaze flicked between Marina and Delaney as she pulled herself to her feet. "Actually, I think the cool night air will do me good."

Turning a sly smile on Delaney, she asked, "You don't mind waiting out front with Marina, do you?"

Marina wondered if he knew just what her friend was up to as they made their way out into the night. The brisk autumn air felt refreshing after the stuffiness of the crowded pub, but being alone with Delaney was doing strange things to the rhythm of her heart.

She looked down the road toward the parking garage. It sure seemed to be taking Erik a long time to bring the car around. When she felt Delaney's gaze on her, she glanced up and shivered at the intensity of his gaze

"You're cold." He shrugged off his sport coat and slipped it around Marina's shoulders.

"Oh, I, uh...thanks," she murmured, catching her bottom lip between her teeth.

Delaney's eyes darted to her lips, quickly flicking away when Marina noticed him staring. The moment he averted his gaze, she dipped her head to inhale the woodsy, mint and citrus scent that clung to his jacket. Closing her eyes, she drew the heady redolence deeper into her lungs, holding it there as long as she could.

Delaney cleared his throat, and her eyes snapped open to find him studying her. He scrubbed a hand over his clean-shaven face. "With all of the business trips I've been on lately, we haven't had much opportunity to talk about, well, I mean--" After a pause he added, "I've noticed you're putting in some long hours at the office."

She knew he wanted to ask how she was coping with her sister's death but he was reluctant to voice it. "I used to spend most of my time with Tasha and Erik." Marina shrugged. "With her gone and Erik finally settled in a committed relationship, I guess I feel a little misplaced." She looked away then, grimacing at how pitiful and lonely she must sound to him.

He'd think her even more pathetic if she were to tell him that she'd been hearing her dead sister's voice. Marina, herself, would have worried more about the state of her mental health had she not read somewhere that hearing the voice of a deceased loved one was actually quite common during the grieving stage. Even so, it wasn't something she was willing to share with others.

"I can understand that." He rubbed at his forehead. "After my wife died—"

Marina's eyes flew to his face. "I-I didn't know."

"Not many people do. I've been pretty closed-lip about it." Delaney shrugged. "Anyway, with no close family members around to share in my grief, I admit to spending an unhealthy amount of time at work. I kept myself so busy, there was little time left over to contemplate my loss. Looking back on it now, I suppose it was cowardly of me to shut all thoughts and memories of Camille out of my life. But it was the only way I knew how to move on."

Her heart lurched, and she wanted to throw her arms around him, to comfort him. Her own parents were still living in denial ten months after the death of their daughter. Fleeing the anguish of Tasha's memory and the surviving daughter who was the living embodiment of her, they'd sold their house and moved across the country to Arizona. Like Grayson, they'd abandoned her to suffer through her grief alone. What kind of parents did that to their child?

Parents who are hurting, Tasha's voice whispered through her head.

But I was hurting, too! Marina thought bitterly. She, herself, had been tempted to jump on the forget-about-Tasha bandwagon and shut her sister out of her mind and heart just as her parents had. She understood now why Delaney had been so good to her. He'd experienced firsthand what it was like to lose a loved one and shoulder the grief on his own. Her heart reached out to his in a silent bond of kinship, intensifying her attraction to him.

"I know what you mean." She nodded. "Those first few months, any thought or mention of Tasha was—" She stopped midsentence, trying to swallow past the sudden lump in her throat, her eyes glistening with un-shed tears.

"I'm sorry." Delaney swore, running a hand through his hair. "I didn't mean to upset you." His unguarded gaze was tender with con-cern. And something else, *longing*? No, she must be imagining things.

"There's nothing to be sorry for." Marina gave a dismissive shake of her head. "I can't thank you enough for everything you've done."

"It's like I told you before," Delaney said softly, "I'm always here for you."

Fleetingly, Marina wished Foster Delaney were anyone but her employer, an ordinary man who could take her in his arms and hold her until all the hurt melted away. But it was futile to yearn for something that would never happen. So she clung to his jacket instead, pulling it tighter around herself while her brain furiously grasped for words to change the topic of conversation.

"I, uh...was surprised to see you here tonight," she blurted out.

Delaney opened his mouth and shut it again, casting a glance toward the parking garage. With a resigned sigh, he finally answered. "Today would've been my fifth wedding anniversary."

"I'm so sorry." Marina instinctively reached out, her hand brushing his arm. It was only the third or fourth time she'd ever had occasion to touch him, but the effect was the same each time. She hastily retracted her hand, trying to absorb the familiar electric shiver that trembled through her.

Delaney's eyes flared at her touch. He stepped back, out of her reach, a frown creasing his forehead. Expelling an audible breath, he swept a hand to the pub behind them. "I needed a distraction from my pity party. This place was close to where I was running errands, so..."

"Oh." Marina tamped down the hurt inflicted by his reaction to her touch. There would be time later to stew over Delaney's rejection. Forcing a smile into her voice, she asked, "Did the distraction work?"

"Yes." A faint smile tugged at one corner of his lips, revealing a single dimple that winked at her. "I believe it did." His eyes locked on hers.

Marina forgot to breathe, unable to tear her eyes away from his. Delaney was the first to break eye contact, a mask of professionalism slipping over his face as Erik's black Nissan Maxima pulled up alongside them. She shrugged out of his jacket and handed it back to him.

"Thank you," she said, climbing into the back seat of the car.

"Good night, Marina."

Before she could respond, Delaney shut her door and hurried across the street.

— ‿ —

Marina blinked away the memory of that night with a dismissive shake of her head. *No*, she reasoned. Their encounter at the pub couldn't possibly be the reason Delaney had asked to see her. After all, nothing improper had occurred.

Unless this concerned her brief gesture of comfort? She recalled the way Delaney had backed away from her touch and experienced a flicker of doubt, but she shook it off. It had been innocent enough, and she was sure Delaney had understood her intent. She tried to convince herself there was nothing to be worried about.

Either way, there was little point in standing outside his door speculating. Squaring her shoulders, Marina prepared to announce herself. Her fist was midair when the door swung open.

"There you are, Marina!" her employer announced loudly, his voice oddly strained.

Was that relief or annoyance she heard in his voice? Marina eyed him suspiciously. First she'd caught her brooding employer lurking outside her office this morning, and now he acted as if he didn't know whether to yank her into his office or send her away. What was up with the mood swings lately? Since that night at the pub, Delaney had fluctuated between cool indifference, cordial formality, and glowering intensity.

"Will you excuse us, Deidra?" he said over his shoulder, pulling the door open wider.

"Of course." Deidra Torres, the office assistant from Argyle's accounting department, appeared in the doorway. Her lush, five-foot-ten figure, hugged in a white wrap dress, revealed a generous peek of cleavage and complemented her smooth, bronzed skin.

"See you...*later*," she purred meaningfully at Delaney, swaying through the narrow space between him and Marina as she exited into the hallway. Deidra's amber, feline glare flicked over Marina haughtily, her pouty lips tugging into an unbecoming sneer as she tossed her voluminous, caramel-colored tresses over her shoulder.

Delaney hooked an index finger in his collar and yanked it side to side, as if it were strangling him. His gaze darted between Marina and Deidra's retreating form as he cleared his throat and swept a hand toward his office. "Please come in."

His voice had returned to its customary professional tone. Marina didn't know what made her more nervous—his discordant greeting a moment ago or his easy switch back to business mode. The butterflies in her stomach fluttered in agitation as Delaney closed the door behind them.

3

Nothing could have prepared Marina for what happened next. "I've arranged for you to take a week's paid vacation." Delaney leaned forward slightly, his arms folding over the shiny mahogany surface of his desk. "Starting tomorrow."

Marina's face felt as if it were frozen in an expression of stunned surprise. Somehow, though, she still managed to form words. "Pardon me?"

Steepling his hands in front of him, Delaney regarded her with solemn green eyes. "After our discussion at the pub last week, I think it's for the best. Don't you?"

She clenched her jaw against a surge of anger, heat pulsing through her veins. *He thinks it's for the best?* Had his thoughtfulness that night been nothing more than a clinical assessment of her mental and emotional health? She could hardly believe it of him. But why was he acting as if he were her psychotherapist all of a sudden?

"Is my work suffering?" she asked coolly.

"Not at all." He made a dismissive gesture and leaned back in his chair. "Your work is exemplary, as usual."

"Then why?" None of this was making any sense to Marina. And how could she just drop everything and go? While it was true that all the time she'd been spending at the office lately had significantly reduced her workload, she was positive she could rustle up something productive to do. "What about the Hiroshi account?"

Delaney stood and walked around the front of the desk to lean casually against one corner. His arms crossed over his pristine blue Armani shirt. "Erik will take care of Hiroshi."

"But—"

"I insist, Marina." Delaney held up a hand to cut her off. "You're spending way too much time at the office, and I can't afford to have my best ad exec get burned out." He pulled a paper from the desktop printer and slid it in front of her.

Marina gave the paper a perfunctory glance, noting only absently a small photo, location map, and some printed information as her employer continued to describe her accommodations.

"You'll be staying at a cabin in Ogunquit." He tapped the paper with his forefinger. "It's equipped with all the modern amenities, including a hot tub out on the deck. This is the perfect time of year to use it, so you might want to take a swimming suit along. He paused, as if gauging her reaction, before adding, "I'm sure you'll love the place as much as I do."

"You've been there?" Marina's brows rose as she watched the paper flutter precariously on the lip of the desk.

"Let's just say I like to know what I'm spending my money on." Delaney shrugged noncommittally, rounding the desk to settle once again in his chair.

"Well, I'm afraid you've wasted your money, Mr. Delaney." She stood, bracing her fingers on the edge of the desk. "I haven't replaced my car yet, so..." She'd sold it to help her parents through the financial hardships brought on by Tasha's treatments, and since she rarely traveled anywhere the bus—or Erik—couldn't take her to, she hadn't felt an overwhelming need to replace it yet.

"That's a nonissue." He waved a hand dismissively. "Everything's been arranged. A car will be around to pick you up tomorrow at ten o'clock sharp. The driver, Mr. Reese, will be staying in the area, and he'll be at your disposal should you wish to visit the coastal towns nearby."

"This seems a bit unorthodox." Marina's eyes narrowed at Delaney. "How many other employees have received this type of company perk?" she asked pointedly, fisting a hand on her hip.

"This is the first. Consider it part of your bonus for the year." He dropped his gaze to some papers on his desk and idly started flipping through them. "Now, if you'll excuse me, Marina, I've got a conference call in just a few minutes."

What, that's it? Marina placed both hands on the desk again and leaned forward. "Sir, I don't understand—"

"Please be ready when the car arrives, Marina." Delaney flashed her a stony this-conversation-is-over glance then turned to peer fixedly at his computer screen.

Bristling at Delaney's curt dismissal, she stalked down the hall, anger and confusion blurring her vision. What was his deal? If her work was so exemplary, as he'd claimed, why was he treating her like an employee in need of a mental health break? She worried, too, about the consequences of accepting inappropriate company perks and stirring up office gossip. Why didn't her employer seem the least bit concerned about the ethical ramifications?

〜 〜

Marina turned a corner and collided with Suki's boyfriend, Milo, from human resources.

A flurry of white envelopes spilled to the ground around them. Hastily, Marina knelt to scoop them up. "Oh, Milo, I'm so sorry!"

"Uh, no problem." His gaze skittered around as if he thought someone might be watching him. A clump of wavy blond hair had fallen over his deep-set blue eyes, and he blew it out of the way. "I'm not sure you would've seen me if I'd been wearing a flashing neon sign." Crouching down beside her, he collected the last of the envelopes. "I called out a warning, but it was like you were in a trance or something."

Marina grimaced. "Sorry. I guess I have a lot on my mind."

"Um, anything I can do to help?" Milo inquired.

"No." She shook her head. "I'll be out of the office for a few days, so I'm sure that will help me clear my head."

"Oh?" He tilted his head in interest. "Going anywhere fun?"

"Not particularly." Her laugh sounded brittle. "Just a remote cabin somewhere up nor—" She stopped abruptly, irritated that she'd inadvertently said more than she'd intended, way more than she should have. The last thing she wanted was to broadcast any details, no matter how small, of her potentially unethical travel arrangements. The only person she felt comfortable discussing this with was Erik, and she made a mental note to do so later.

"Oh, I almost forgot..." He helped her to her feet. "Suki's looking for you." He scuffed his foot on the carpet. "Said something about a surprise you were helping her with for our date on Friday?" he prompted, tapping the stack of envelopes against the palm of his hand in a quick staccato.

"I'll go look for her now." Marina nodded. "Thanks, Milo."

"Sure." He stood there expectantly, as if waiting for her to divulge more information. "Well, uh...enjoy your time off," he finally muttered, waving awkwardly as he backed down the hall.

She shook her head as she watched him disappear around a corner. She didn't understand what Suki saw in Milo. She'd heard women in the office refer to him as a "hot nerd," but to her he was mostly nerdy. Marina supposed his personality was likable enough, although he did seem a little high-strung lately. On that thought, an image of Milo's agitated conversation with Deidra at the summer kickoff party popped into her head, but she quickly brushed it away. It was probably nothing. Besides, the important thing was that Suki seemed perfectly content in her relationship with Milo.

Marina wished she could find that level of fulfillment in her own relationships with men. Well, actually, with one man in particular. She couldn't help wondering what it would be like to be in a committed relationship with Delaney, whose gem-colored eyes changed from the verdant green of Irish moss in bright light to a misty gray-green in shadow. Just thinking about his dimples was enough to scramble her thoughts and turn her knees to jelly. And what would it be like if he touched his lips to hers? She'd allowed herself to imagine his kiss more times than she should. But the images flooding her head now went way beyond a chaste peck on the lips. No, these fantasies involved Delaney's mouth caressing the most intimate parts of her body.

A wave of heat shot through her, and Marina covered her cheeks with her hands. Did her face burn as red-hot as the rest of her body? She hurried toward the ladies' room at the far end of the hall, desperate to splash her face with cool water before Suki, or any of her other coworkers, saw the state she was in.

Dashing past the copy room on her right, she skidded to a halt as she recognized the cloying drawl of Deidra's voice. "Delaney said he was only meeting with me because Sheila from human resources is out sick today." Her voice lowered conspiratorially. "But we both know he just wanted to get me in his office, *alone*."

"Oh, yeah," a female voice answered. "He is *soooo* into you."

Marina plastered herself against the wall outside the copy room door. The ladies' room was kitty-corner from where she now stood. She should march right in there and ignore what she'd heard. But the mention of Delaney's name had seized her attention and rooted her to the spot, as if her feet were cemented to the floor.

"I know, right?" Deidra was saying. "I'm telling you, the man couldn't keep his eyes off me, and I could tell he wanted his hands all over me, too."

Marina's breath hitched as she caught her bottom lip between her teeth. She'd never thought of Foster Delaney as the type of employer to engage in inappropriate workplace dalliances. As far as she knew, he was the kind of man who'd deny himself the companionship of a woman if it meant damaging professional relationships, tarnishing reputations, or deviating from office decorum.

"So...what happened?" The other woman's question wrenched Marina from her thoughts.

"We were interrupted," Deidra responded in a pouty voice.

Her companion sighed in apparent disappointment. "Well, that sucks."

"Oh, I'm sure we'll have no trouble picking up right where we left off," Deidra murmured.

Marina didn't like the husky promise in the woman's voice. She shuddered to think just where Deidra and her employer had "left off." Shaking the disturbing thought aside, she turned her attention back to the conversation.

"Anyway, I don't have long to wait. He wants to meet me tomorrow after work." Deidra's voice took on a smug tone. "And we both know what that means."

Marina frowned. Delaney's obvious discomfort as she'd observed Deidra leaving his office earlier seemed to support everything she'd just heard. Was it possible she didn't know her employer as well as she thought? Admittedly, she knew Deidra even less, but she couldn't imagine why the woman would fabricate such a thing.

All Marina knew for sure was that she couldn't listen to another word. Launching herself across the hall into the ladies' room, she splashed her face several times with cool water and patted it dry with a paper towel.

Inspecting her reflection in the mirror, she glimpsed a pair of royal-blue stilettos underneath one of the stalls. *Well, crap,* Marina mouthed the words to her mirror image. She was in no mood to face anyone right now. But before she could make her escape, the toilet flushed, and the stall door swung open.

"Hey, I was just coming to look for you!"

"Suki!" Marina heaved a sigh of relief, trying to return her friend's smile but managing only a weak half grin that was mostly a grimace.

Exotic, almond-shaped eyes narrowed at her. "Are you all right?"

Marina hesitated. Suki was the closest thing to a female friend she had at Argyle, and she desperately needed to confide in someone about what she'd heard outside the copy room. She still planned to discuss it with Erik, of course, but sometimes a gal just needed to talk to another woman about these things.

If only Tasha were still around! How she missed being able to call her big sister whenever she needed advice. In the absence of a trusted sister, should she confide in Suki? While she was fairly certain she could trust the woman, she had no wish to inadvertently spread rumors about Delaney—or herself, for that matter—whether they were true or not. Perhaps it was best, for now at least, to keep Deidra's conversation to herself.

"Marina?"

Suki's voice dragged Marina from her thoughts. "Oh, yeah." She nodded dismissively. "I'm good."

Giving her a wary look, Suki nodded and moved over to the sink. "Are you sure you want to loan me your dress?" she asked Marina's reflection as she washed her hands. "I mean, it's so gorgeous, and it's practically brand new, and—"

"And"—Marina handed her a paper towel— "it will be perfect for the art gala. The poor thing's just been sitting in my closet gathering dust." Tasha had insisted on purchasing the aqua-blue evening gown when she learned her little sister hadn't packed anything suitable for a night of wining, dining, and dancing in Puerto Rico. But Marina had never worn the dress again after their vacation. She supposed it was partially because the garment reminded her that Tasha was no longer around. Mostly, though, Marina felt supremely ridiculous wearing anything so glamorous. Jill was right about her after all. She was a business casual gal, preferring tailored garments that were simple and classy, without being flashy.

"I don't know." Suki's lips turned down at the corners, and she lowered her eyebrows. "What if I accidentally ruin it somehow?"

"You won't." Marina gave her shoulder a reassuring pat. Grinning, she added, "Besides, poor Milo is dying of curiosity."

Twin blooms of color stained Suki's alabaster cheeks. "You're right." She smiled wistfully, her dark brown eyes unfocused with the glow of new love. "Milo will love it."

"'Atta girl." Marina linked arms with Suki, all thoughts of Deidra and Delaney momentarily forgotten. "Let's go back to my office and get your dress."

— —

After Suki left, Marina shut the door and closed the blinds that scaled the floor-to-ceiling glass walls of her office. She craved peace and quiet after what had been an inordinately eventful day. Settling back against the desk chair, she let her eyes drift shut. Almost immediately, Marina's thoughts wandered back to Foster Delaney.

What was going on with him, anyway? Since their conversation at the pub the previous weekend, she'd watched Delaney struggle to maintain an air of polished professionalism, noticing subtle cracks in his unflappable exterior.

Today, his behavior had boomeranged all over the place, from the intense expression on his face when she'd caught him watching her earlier in the morning to his restive temperament as Deidra had left his office. And what about the impromptu vacation he'd sprung on her, followed by his rather curt dismissal?

Did Deidra Torres have something to do with Delaney's curious behavior, or was that merely coincidental? Was her mandatory vacation his way of putting distance between them, because he'd discovered Marina's feelings for him? It seemed unlikely when there were far more practical methods of dealing with such matters.

As confusing as it all was, Marina had to admit that putting a little distance between herself and Delaney was probably a good idea. She didn't have the energy to deal with his shifting moods when she was already struggling to suppress her very-non-professional feelings for him. With any luck, her absence would improve his attitude. If not, she'd be forced to confront him before his behavior made working at Argyle intolerable.

And Marina couldn't let that happen. This job was her lifeline, and she had no intention of leaving anytime soon.

4

It was nearing six o'clock that evening when Erik poked his dark head through Marina's office door.

"Did someone kill a clown in here?" He plopped into a chair in front of her desk. "Because you *do not* look happy."

"Apparently, I'm being forced to take a paid vacation for no reason at all other than Delaney demands it."

"Poor baby." Erik clucked his tongue.

"I should be saying that to you." Marina slanted him a sympathetic smile. "You get to handle the Hiroshi account while I'm gone."

Though his jaw visibly slackened, Erik waved off her news admirably. "Not to worry. I'll have him eating sushi out of my hands by the time you get back."

Marina snickered at his joke. But she sobered quickly, her brows crinkling into a frown. "Erik, have you heard of any of the other ad execs receiving paid vacation perks?"

"Don't know, Rina." He grabbed a piece of candy from the jar on her desk and popped it in his mouth. "What's bothering you?"

"It's just that..." Marina nibbled at her bottom lip. "Well, I don't want to do anything, you know...inappropriate."

"You?" Erik smirked. "Not likely." But his expression softened. "Don't worry, Rina. Delaney always has a good reason for everything he does. Have you ever known him to do anything that was controversial or improper?"

"Not that I can think of," Marina conceded.

"Well, there you go." Erik gave the desk two solid taps with his index finger.

She nodded, nipping at her bottom lip again.

"If you keep eating those gorgeous lips of yours, there won't be anything left for the guys." Erik waggled his brows at her.

Marina frowned, immediately releasing her lip. It was a nervous habit that had manifested itself during Tasha's illness and had, to her dismay, increased in frequency since her sister's death. "I was just wondering what the heck I'm going to do camped out at a remote cabin for a whole week."

"I believe the idea is to relax, Rina." He settled back against the chair he occupied. "I'll even take care of Her Majesty the Queen, so there's nothing you need to worry about here."

She smiled at his reference to the rather aloof feline who shared her condo and typically only acknowledged Marina's existence if her food bowl lacked sustenance. Whenever Erik was about, however, the cat would preen and posture shamelessly for his attention, not unlike the stream of women he'd dated before Jill. Erik had always had a way with the ladies. Her own luck with the opposite sex had been somewhat less charmed, but she wasn't about to preen and posture for any man. She'd leave that to Her Majesty, thank you very much.

Maybe, if she expended as much energy trying to meet other men as she did trying to conceal her feelings for her employer, she might actually have a chance of finding a nice guy. It was hard to imagine that happening, though. As long as Delaney owned real estate in her heart, there was no room for anyone else to move in. The thought strengthened her resolve to use her upcoming hiatus from Argyle as a new beginning, a chance to convince her head, and her heart, that it was time to move on.

Maybe Delaney was doing her a favor after all by forcing her to take time off.

"So, out of sheer curiosity..." Erik leaned forward and rested his arms on her desk. "What do you think of Delaney, anyway?"

"He's been a good employer." Marina tried to school her voice with what she hoped sounded like appropriate respect for a colleague, but she was afraid it was coming off a bit hollow.

"What I meant was," he enunciated each word, "what do you think of him, you know, as a man?"

"I've always thought very highly of him." Marina leaned back in her seat, her thumb clicking the pen in her hand in a succession of rapid taps. "But lately..." she hesitated. "Well, I've heard some things that, for the first time, make me question my opinion of him."

Erik plucked the pen away from her. "I don't know what you've heard, but you've never been the type to pay attention to gossip before." He gave her a pointed look that shamed her. "Delaney's one of the most decent guys I know."

Marina resumed her lip biting.

"You're doing that thing again," Erik admonished.

She released her lips with a huff of irritation. "I know."

"That you shouldn't be biting your lips or that you shouldn't listen to gossip?"

"Both," Marina grumbled.

"Have I managed to restore your good opinion of Delaney, then?"

"I guess," she replied lamely.

"Good, because I want to throw a hypothetical at you."

"I'm not sure I want to hear it," she shot back, leveling him with her most intimidating scowl.

"Oh, settle down." Erik waved away her reaction and forged ahead anyway. "What would you say if I were to tell you that Delaney is totally crushing on you?"

Marina's heart flip-flopped in her chest, even as she speared Erik with an irritated glare. "Don't be ridiculous, Erik."

"It's no more ridiculous than you wasting seven months of your life on that jerk Grayson." He wrinkled his nose as if he'd just smelled something disgusting.

"Did I mention that he called again?"

"What?" Erik scowled murderously. "Did he leave a message this time?"

"Nope, he just lets the dumb phone ring a dozen times then hangs up."

"Give it to me." He held out his hand.

Marina fished the device out of her purse and plopped it in his hand. The phone beeped a few times as he scrolled through the settings and punched several buttons.

"There." Erik handed the phone back to her with a satisfied smirk. "Let the douchebag try and get through now."

"Thanks." She tossed the phone back in her handbag.

"As I was saying, before the subject of Grayson so rudely interrupted our pleasant conversation..." He brushed at the lapels of his suit coat, as if flicking away the distasteful subject of her ex. "Delaney's got it bad for you. And before you remind me again that he's your employer, let me remind *you* that he's also a man who's in desperate need of a woman. And the woman he happens to want is *you*."

"I'm afraid to ask"— she rubbed at her forehead— "but how do you presume to know that, exactly?"

"A guy can just tell when another guy has it bad for a woman." Erik's cocky expression betrayed his casual shrug.

"That's totally irrelevant." Marina's laugh was short and humorless. "He's my employer. Nothing, hypothetical or otherwise, can happen between us." She'd known it all along, had thought about it often. But somehow, saying the words out loud just now made it seem glaringly real, concrete, and final. Suddenly, she couldn't wait to be away from the office, to distance herself from Delaney and everything that reminded her of him.

Unfortunately, Erik had other ideas.

"Well, you might be able to blow off my man-tuition, but my gypsy mojo will not be denied. And you know what it's telling me?"

When she opened her mouth to answer, he held up a hand. "That was a rhetorical question, Rina." Twining two of his fingers together, he said meaningfully, "You and Delaney belong together."

Marina's eyes widened as a disturbing thought popped into her head. "Is that why you forced the poor man to dance with me at the summer kickoff party?"

"Believe me," he assured her. "There was *no* forcing."

"Whatever." She snorted. "Save your gypsy matchmaking services for the rest of the girls in the office." She hated it when Erik played the gypsy card. Just because he was one-quarter Romany didn't mean he'd actually inherited a sixth sense from his great-grandmother. As far as she was concerned, his supposed psychic abilities, as he liked to call them, amounted to nothing more than hunches, coincidences, and superstition.

Never mind that she wished his hunches were true. She rather liked the idea of belonging to Delaney. But it was impossible. He had a strict company policy against executives or anyone in a managerial position dating employees. Erik knew it, too. So why would he even bring up Delaney's alleged feelings for her?

"I'm not hearing any complaints from *them*," he pointed out with a self-satisfied tone. "In fact, Suki and Milo seem pretty happy with my services."

It was true, she grudgingly acknowledged the fact. The couple had started dating several weeks prior to the summer kickoff party in May, after Erik had convinced Milo to ask Suki on a date. And now, whenever the urge to doubt Erik's metaphysical gifts struck her, he took it upon himself to regale her with tales of his frequent matchmaking successes. She was tempted to pointedly remind him that Jill had eluded his gypsy mojo long enough to make him question his Romany gifts, but right now she wanted nothing more than to escape this conversation.

"Don't you have any work to do?" she hinted with a suggestive brow.

"Let's see..." Erik started ticking things off with his fingers. "I single-handedly closed the Fenton account, managed to torment Delaney with my clever verbal banter, *and* thoroughly cleaned my desk. So, um...no."

"Well, I do," Marina grumbled, making a show of shuffling some folders on her desk. "It's late. Go home to your fiancée." She crumpled a piece of paper in her hands and threw it at him.

"Damn, you're cranky." Erik caught the little ball in his large, brown hands, playfully tossing it back her way as he ducked out of the office.

Marina smiled indulgently at his antics, sweeping notepads into a neat pile, pens into a drawer, and folders into their designated files in preparation for her absence. She was startled when Erik's broad frame reappeared in the doorway, his penetrating black gaze boring into hers.

"Promise to think about what I said while you're on vacation, OK?"

She grimaced. Thinking about Delaney was the last thing she intended to do while she was away. But she plastered a smile on her face and offered her friend a reassuring nod as she shooed him away with a flick of her manicured fingers.

Absently, she arranged her stapler and pen holder, her eyes roaming over the cheerful daisy and ivory rose bouquet on her desk. She'd forgotten to ask Erik to water it for her while she was gone, and since she hated to see a good daisy bouquet go to waste, she pulled out her cell and texted him, suggesting he take it home to Jill, who had been under the weather since their dinner at the pub the previous weekend. With a click of her mouse, the dolphin wallpaper on her computer screen faded to black. She slid into her coat, snatched up her purse, and pulled the door shut behind her.

— —

With deliberate strides, Marina hurried down the hall to the bank of elevators. It would be after seven before she made it home, and her head was spinning with everything she had to get done before her impromptu vacation in the morning. She'd probably need most of the night just to get her blasted suitcase packed. Unlike Tasha, who could have made a living as a professional speed-packer, Marina had never been any good at it.

Stepping into an empty elevator, she turned to punch the button for the main floor lobby and glimpsed Milo exiting the hall she'd just vacated. He looked around furtively, swiping at the sheen of sweat glistening on his forehead. Before the elevator doors closed, Milo's gaze met hers. Turning away, he darted out of sight. *Poor guy looks stressed,* Marina thought with sympathy. *He must be overloaded with projects to be here so late.*

As the elevator made its descent, she leaned against the wall, her eyes closing of their own volition. She was surprised at the weariness settling over her. As much as it irritated her to admit Delaney had been right, there was no denying the way her body felt.

She *did* need a vacation.

— ⁓

Marina peered at the empty suitcase and the jumble of clothing strewn across her bed. She shoved aside a pile of garments and sank onto the mattress. If she were going on a business trip, packing would've been a cinch. As it was, she found herself staring absently at the monstrous pile of clothes, recalling how she'd done the exact same thing when she'd packed for her trip to Puerto Rico two years before. Finally, at two o'clock in the morning on the day of departure, she'd given up and settled on several pairs of tailored slacks, a few fitted blouses, a lightweight jacket, and one delicately flared skirt. She could still vividly remember Tasha's incredulous snort of disapproval.

"Are you serious, Mari?" she'd groaned. "You're vacationing in a Caribbean paradise, *chica*. Dress like it!" Needless to say, Tasha had insisted they spend their first day in Puerto Rico shopping. Marina swallowed past the lump in her throat, wishing Tasha were going with her now. But she wasn't, and the suitcase wasn't filling itself.

Hauling herself back to her feet, she sifted through her closet. Her fingers brushed across the outfits they'd purchased in Puerto Rico, and she pursed her lips, considering. She was at a complete loss as to what to wear beyond her business casual outfits and just plain tired of debating what to pack. Extracting the teal-colored knit shirt, distressed boyfriend jeans, flowing native-print maxi skirt, and gauzy, embroidered tunic, she neatly folded them into her suitcase, along with a shirt dress, pair of slacks, and her white silk blouse. In addition to a pair of comfortable flats, she added her equestrian boots, her favorite gray blazer, and a loose-fitting cashmere sweater, along with her worn nightshirt and a nearly threadbare terrycloth robe. On a whim, she tossed in the cozy novelty slippers—with doggy faces and big, floppy ears—that Tasha had given her as a joke the Christmas before she died.

A sudden streak of gray flew past her with a frenzied snarl, eliciting a yip of surprise from Marina. Back arched, Her Majesty stood in the suitcase, hissing and clawing at the doggy slippers.

"You scared me, you silly beast!" Marina extracted the grumbling ball of fur and set her on the floor. "Patience, Majesty." Marina rolled her eyes at the big gray cat. "As of tomorrow, you'll be rid of me and the slippers for a whole week." The cat tilted her head, ears pricked in interest.

"Erik's going to drop by every day to check on you and make sure you're fed."

Purring her approval, the feline gave Marina a haughty flick of her tail before curling up under the whicker chair in the corner of the room.

"Yeah," Marina snorted. "That's what I thought." She had half a mind to give the silly beast to Erik. It had really never seemed to care for her much anyway. She'd taken the animal only on the request of a neighbor who'd been forced to move and desperately wanted to find a good home for her feline friend.

Her cell phone clicked and whistled as she was zipping up her suitcase, and Marina picked it up, staring in mute astonishment at the number on her screen. Her parents were calling. First Grayson and now this? Why were the people who'd abandoned her when she needed them most suddenly reaching out to her? She didn't know what they wanted, but she wasn't prepared to deal with it. Letting the call go to voice mail, Marina shoved aside thoughts of her parents and struggled to remember if there was something she was forgetting.

It occurred to her then that she still hadn't packed her swimming suit. Much like the dress she'd loaned to Suki, the iridescent blue one-piece, with metal accents, was a little too flashy for her taste, not to mention slightly more revealing than she cared for. After a few moments of deliberation, she gave in.

"Oh, what the heck." She tucked the swimming suit into a mesh pocket. "Who's going to see me in it?" Besides, as Delaney had informed her, she was going on vacation, and it would be silly of her not to enjoy all the amenities the cabin had to offer while she was there.

Delaney.

The man had an uncanny ability to slip into her thoughts. "Well, that just won't do." Marina swept her arms around the room in a wide arch. "I declare this room a Delaney-free zone!"

Her Majesty sniffed loudly, as if to say, *Good luck with that.*

"I know." Marina blew a raspberry at the cat. "I'll be lucky if I can get through the rest of the night without that irritating man popping into my head."

And she was right.

The irritating man in question haunted her dreams all through the night.

By the time the sun peeked through her windows Thursday morning, Marina was already yanking back the bed covers and tumbling from the mattress. Not only was she on a mission to enjoy her break from work, but she also planned to take a serious vacation from any and all thoughts of Foster Delaney.

When the black limo pulled up in front of her condo at precisely ten o'clock, she was waiting at the curb with her luggage.

5

"Good morning." The chauffeur's pale blue eyes twinkled merrily as he tipped his cap, revealing a glimpse of silver hair. "You must be Miss Thatcher."

The warmth of his smile echoed in his voice, and Marina was immediately taken with him. His face, wizened by a feathering of lines along his forehead, around his lips, and at the corners of his eyes, made him look distinguished rather than elderly. "Mr. Reese, is it?"

"Just Reese will do." He flashed her a conspiratorial grin as he helped her into the limousine. "You'll find a package from Mr. Delaney in the center console of your seat. I'll just get your luggage loaded, and we'll be underway."

When he'd shut her door, Marina lifted the lid of the console, her eyes widening when they fell upon the box inside. It was wrapped in exquisitely designed paper with a Japanese flower motif. Had Delaney purchased it on one of his many business trips over the summer? To think he'd thought of her while he was away caused a peculiar flutter in her heart.

Marina slammed the console shut when the driver's side door opened. She propped an elbow upon it, casually kneading her earlobe between her fingers.

Reese gave her a curious look in the rearview mirror. "Just sit back, relax, and enjoy the ride," he suggested with a half smile.

But she didn't.

All Marina could think about the whole trip was the darn gift box. As far as she knew, there was no company culture for gift giving at Argyle, not even during the holidays. And that made her worry about the intent of the gift. Was it relevant to her professional relationship with Delaney? Was it considered part of her bonus vacation, or had he given everyone in the office the same gift? No, she decided. If that were the case, the box would surely bear the Argyle logo.

She stared out the window at the passing scenery trying to distract herself from her thoughts, but even the beauty of the coastal scenery along Rt. 9 couldn't hold her attention. Her fingers absently traced a lazy pattern on the console lid, her mind lost in speculation over the purpose of the box inside. Even if there was nothing intrinsically wrong with her employer giving her a gift, she feared it would weaken her ability to remain impartial to him when she was already struggling to keep her personal feelings for him under control for the sake of their professional relationship.

Marina rubbed at her temples and leaned her head back against the leather seat. She'd thought wrestling with her doubts over accepting an all-expenses-paid vacation as a legitimate company perk had been difficult. But for some reason, it was nothing compared to the turmoil she was experiencing over the box hidden in the console.

Turning onto a private wooded drive bordered on either side by tall birch trees ablaze with vibrant leaves in harvest red, squash yellow, and burnt orange, Marina sighed in contentment.

Fall had always been her favorite season, and the splendor of warm autumn colors lifted her spirits. When they pulled up in front of the sprawling, two-story cabin and she stepped out of the limo, the air smelled of wood smoke and the spicy musk of decaying leaves. Her gaze

swept over the lawn, manicured to retain as much of the natural landscape as possible, stretching out to meet the surrounding woods. A small
smile curved her mouth. It was just the type of place she imagined one
would come to escape from the cares of everyday life, and heaven knew
she needed a reprieve from the burden of caring, more than she should,
for her employer.

"Oh, Miss Thatcher!" Reese's voice broke through her thoughts. "I
believe you forgot this." He walked purposefully to her side, the object
she'd tried to forget about on the drive to Ogunquit cradled in his extended hand.

The gift box.

Marina stared at it as if it were a snake ready to strike.

"I always double-check the limo for items clients might uninten-
tionally leave behind."

Of course he did, she thought with a wry half smile. "Oh, uh, thank you."
She plucked the box from his hand and hastily stuffed it into her purse.
Clearing her throat, Marina arched a brow at Reese, who'd just retrieved
her bags from the limo's trunk. "Are you sure we're at the right place?"
She eyed the Taj-Malodge in front of her dubiously.

He pulled a paper from his pocket and unfolded it. As he did so,
Marina noted that it looked similar to the one Delaney had shown her
in his office, with some additional scribbled notes that appeared to be
her name and address in Portland. Reese skimmed the paper and peered
up at the luxury cabin looming before them. "Looks like it, miss." He
smiled at her reassuringly. "Let's get you settled."

Marina cast a sidelong glance at the chauffeur as they walked the
short distance to the cabin's front door. "Does Mr. Delaney have you
bring his employees up here often?"

"Don't know, Miss Thatcher." Reese slid the key into the locking
mechanism and pushed open the door. "This is my first month with
Mr. Delaney. I'm mighty grateful to him for the work, with my wife sick
and all."

She grimaced. The last thing Marina wanted to hear was another
story of her employer's generosity. It would serve only to endear him to

her further, an obstacle she didn't need when she was trying to use this vacation to accomplish just the reverse.

"You'll be staying in the master suite upstairs," Reese was saying as he guided her through a brief tour of the cabin.

Marina nodded absently. The place was huge. A small, one-room cottage would have suited her just as well. What had Delaney been thinking to rent a cabin this size for one person? A game room in the loft area upstairs separated the two guest suites. The main floor boasted a chef-worthy kitchen, equipped with stainless steel appliances; a study; sauna; and vaulted great room. Down the hall from the kitchen, past the full bath, was a set of closed double doors fitted with an electronic keypad.

"That's the owner's private suite," Reese supplied when she stopped in front of them.

"Oh." Marina nodded. She didn't know why it surprised her. It was perfectly reasonable for homeowners in resort areas to rent out their residences to vacationers when not staying there themselves.

I'm sure you'll love it as much as I do.

Delaney's words flitted through her mind, and her face scrunched into a frown. Where had that come from? True, Delaney had mentioned being here, but that hardly suggested he owned the place. Besides, the man rarely left the office, except when he was on a business trip. It would be a waste of money to invest in such an exorbitant luxury if one had little occasion to use it. Marina pushed the random thought from her head and hustled to catch up with Reese, who had moved on down the hall without her.

He pointed out the large hot tub, visible through the sliding-glass doors off the dining area. At the front of the house, off the great room, was a patio furnished with an inviting set of cushioned wicker furniture. The interior of the cabin was immaculately maintained, with expensive-looking, modern rustic furnishings and a big-screen TV mounted above the huge stone fireplace. Again, Marina was struck by how much the rental must have cost, leaving her to wonder all over again why Delaney wasted such extravagance on an employee.

"The pantry and fridge are fully stocked." Reese gestured toward the kitchen with a sweep of his arm. "But I'm more than happy to drive you into town, should you require anything at all." Holding up an index finger, he added, "Oh, and there's a golf cart in the garage you can use to drive the trail around the grounds. I enjoy the walk myself, but I'll show you where the key is, and you can use it at your leisure."

"I prefer to walk, too." Marina smiled, rummaging through her purse. Pulling out a twenty-dollar bill, she held it out to the chauffeur. "Thank you, Reese."

"Oh, that won't be necessary, miss." He shook his head, handing her his card instead.

"Please call me Marina." She took the card he proffered.

"If you'd like." He nodded affably, his eyes glittering with the jolly twinkle he'd first greeted her with earlier that morning. "Enjoy your stay, Miss—I mean, Marina."

She watched as the limo disappeared down the dirt and gravel drive. The city seemed a million miles away from this secluded coastal woodland area. She wondered if Delaney was as relieved to have her out of the office as she was to be away from it.

"Ugh!" Why was she still thinking about him? She had a vacation to enjoy, and her employer had no place in it. Closing the cabin door purposefully, as if it could somehow shut out thoughts of Delaney, she placed Reese's card by the cordless phone in the kitchen and went to unpack.

— —

Twilight had faded into darkness when Marina settled into the frothy warmth of the hot tub, her mind wandering back over the events of the afternoon.

After unpacking her things, she'd lazily meandered through the cabin, familiarizing herself with each room. Her own suite was practically larger than the entire living area of her condo in Portland. The walls were a blend of timber and painted surfaces, with a king-sized bed, sitting area, and a bathroom that resembled those she'd seen in some five-star hotels.

Vases of white daisies, with cheerful yellow centers, graced the dresser, sitting table, and night stands, while accents in sea-mist-blue and soft yellow, including several ocean and sea-life themed wall pieces, gave the room a serene coastal vibe.

One picture in particular had captivated her, a photo of two dolphins arcing through the air, their sleek, gray bodies glistening in the bright sun as they poised to dive back into the Caribbean-blue sea side by side. She'd been fascinated with the animals since she was a child, and the picture provided her with a measure of familiar comfort.

She'd spared the game room only a cursory glance as she passed it on her way to the staircase. Descending to the first floor, she'd instinctively gravitated toward the study. Moving about the room, she noted the distinct masculinity of the furnishings, the dark leather chairs and black, executive-style desk with carved leather panels and nail-head trim. Three picture windows lined the back wall, with French doors exiting onto the wraparound porch. Built-in bookshelves lined the entire wall to her left, with literary classics by some of her favorite authors—Alexander Dumas and Edgar Rice Burroughs.

She smiled as her fingers brushed along the bindings of what looked to be the entire *Tarzan* series. Tasha had read several of the books to her when she was ten years old, assuming different voices for each character. Marina had found herself magically transported to Africa, vividly living each adventure in her mind's eye.

"Well, whoever owns this place..." she said, swiping the *Tarzan of the Apes* novel from the shelf to read later, "they certainly have good taste in literature." She tapped her index finger against her pursed lips, recalling the sunny, daisy bouquets and arresting dolphin picture hanging in her suite. "And flowers. And art."

When her stomach had started grumbling, she'd headed into the kitchen to see about fixing lunch. Marina opened the stainless steel fridge, and her eyes widened appreciatively. Reese hadn't been kidding about the kitchen being well stocked. The fridge was practically an entire grocery store in and of itself, and she pulled out the fixings for a sandwich.

She ate lunch on the patio under the lazy autumn sun then reclined on the wicker sofa where she browsed several magazines she'd brought with her. Later, she'd strolled along the paved trail that separated the cabin's lawns from the forest beyond. Golden beams of sunlight filtered through the leaves and branches as she wandered around to the backyard, where she came upon the head of a narrow footpath that ambled off through the trees.

Marina took a few tentative steps along the path, squinting through the foliage for any signs as to where it might lead. Glancing up at the late afternoon sun, she retraced her steps. The footpath would have to wait for another day when there was more daylight to explore it. Turning, she followed the mossy stone pavers, passing through the backyard's shady gardens, which were filled with woodland wildflowers and feathery ferns. Then she climbed the deck stairs to skirt around the covered hot tub, and she entered the house through the sliding-glass doors.

She'd wondered, fleetingly, how Erik was handling the Hiroshi account as she absently wandered through the house. But she quickly shook off the thought. No way was she going to think about work...because that would invariably lead to thinking of Delaney.

Inexplicably, Marina had found herself in front of the closed double doors, down the main hallway from the kitchen. She stared at the brushed nickel door handles, her teeth nipping at her bottom lip as she considered what it was about the place that so piqued her curiosity about its owner. Her hands followed the trail of her thoughts, reaching out to jostle the door handles. Snapping her hands back, she'd furtively glanced around as if an unseen pair of eyes might catch her snooping.

After dinner, she browsed the selection of DVDs in the great room, thinking to entertain herself with a movie on the big-screen TV. But she felt unaccountably restless. Thoughts of the gift box, still tucked away in her purse, hovered in the back of her mind. Not even *Tarzan of the Apes* had succeeded at keeping her distracted.

Finally, Marina had changed into her swimming suit and headed out to the deck, where she now willed the thermal eddies of the hot tub to ease away her nervous energy.

Her first day at the cabin had revealed to Marina a truth she'd previously been unable to admit to herself. She'd forgotten how to enjoy life's simple pleasures in the midst of her grief. While she'd been aware of her growing tendency to spend more and more time at work since Tasha's death, she hadn't realized just how much of her life had been consumed by it. With the exception of Erik's social interventions, her daily routine had become a series of mundane wash-rinse-repeat tasks that had merely served to keep her functioning but did little to bring her pleasure or joy.

A cool breeze whispered across Marina's face, kissing the tops of her bare shoulders. Her eyes drifted open to the incredible sight of thousands of stars twinkling against the dark canopy of the sky, and her breath hitched at the simple beauty of it. Tasha would've loved this. Of course, she'd also be annoyed by how Marina had denied herself such experiences over the past ten months. Even with terminal cancer, Tasha had somehow managed to live with passion and enthusiasm.

A flicker of shame flashed through Marina. She had a fulfilling career, a great condo, and friends who truly cared for her. Plus, she was in excellent health. She should be enjoying the blessings of each day instead of muddling through the hours in a haze of perpetual mourning over the loss of her sister and self-pity over her unrequited feelings for Delaney. As if in agreement with her inner reflections, the leaves rustled in the night breeze, bringing Tasha's voice to her ears.

That's it, Mari...embrace life, and let it heal you .The healing will lead you back to Mom and Dad.

Marina shook her head. While she was willing to make a greater effort at embracing life again, she didn't think she was ready to reconcile with her parents yet. The wounds of their neglect and abandonment were still too raw. Pushing aside thoughts of her estranged parents, she closed her eyes, and her mind drifted aimlessly as the bubbling warmth of the water's caress massaged away her cares.

— ~

Marina's eyes snapped open at the sharp crack of breaking twigs and the distinct *crunch-crunch-crunch* of brittle leaves.

All her senses were on full alert, and her heart thumped erratically. Squinting through the dim lights illuminating the perimeter of the hot tub, she barely made out the shadowy form separating itself from the darkness beyond the deck.

She blinked hard.

Surely she was imagining the wolflike beast slowly advancing toward the deck, its yellow eyes glowing ominously in the blackness of night.

Sinister eyes that were fixed upon *her*.

Did wolves even exist in Maine? Marina was pretty sure she wasn't going to live long enough to find out.

The creature was already lunging for her.

6

The animal plunged into the water, sending a wave across the hot tub that splashed Marina full in the face. Choking out a mouthful of chlorinated water, she shoved away the wet hair plastered to her face.

Swiping a hand over her stinging blurry eyes, she scrambled from the jetted spa. She'd barely stepped onto the deck when she heard something else crash through the trees behind her. *Run!* her mind screamed.

But fear paralyzed her, freezing her to the spot.

"Hawk!" a male voice boomed. "Come!"

Marina heard a cacophony of splashing noises and swiped at her eyes again. A shiver of relief ran through her when she saw the dog's large form bound out of the hot tub, and away from her. It paused to shake itself off, wagged its tail, and trotted down the deck stairs to the tall, waiting shadow.

"Did ya have a good swim, boy?" The amusement in the man's voice was unmistakable. "Oh, uh...sorry about that," he amended, addressing her contritely.

"Y-your dog likes hot tubs?" Marina stuttered, trying to make out the man's features in the dim light. Flashes of moonlight illuminated his broad shoulders and muscled arms, but with his back to the moon, his face was obscured in darkness.

"What male doesn't enjoy a woman in a hot tub?"

His throaty chuckle was as disarming as his delicious, Southern drawl. Fleetingly, Marina found herself wondering what had brought a Southern gentleman all the way to Maine. Then she quickly reminded herself that she should probably be worried about talking to a total stranger—one who had a large dog as a companion—at night in an isolated area. Not that there was anything threatening in his demeanor to make her fear him. He hadn't even tried to approach her. Still, one could never be too careful.

"Where did you come from?" Marina took a step back, her gaze bouncing between the man, the dog, and the dark forest beyond. "I mean, do you, uh..."

"Live around here?" he supplied for her.

She nodded even though, in the dim light, he probably didn't notice.

"There's a path back there that leads to my cabin," he said from the shadows. Marina thought she saw his body shift slightly toward the wooded fringe outlining the backyard. "We walk by here fairly often, but it's usually empty."

"A-are you..." She shivered in the brisk air. "A year-round resident here, then?"

"Sometimes," he replied vaguely.

Marina pursed her lips at his cryptic answer. The sudden lull in conversation intensified as moonbeams sifted through a patch of cloud cover to flicker over her swimsuit-clad body. Feeling his eyes upon her, she sucked in a breath and snatched the towel from the deck railing, tightly wrapping it around her body.

"Well, I uh...guess we'd best be going." The man in the shadows cleared his throat. "Sorry again about turnin' your Jacuzzi into a doggy bath."

Her gaze darted nervously around the moon-silvered yard. "Does he—Hawk, I mean—wander this way often?" Marina struggled to maintain a steady voice. She hadn't been overly fond of dogs since that day in April when a Pomeranian had latched onto her ankle while she was out on her morning jog. Luckily, Erik had been with her and had used his gypsy magic to force the animal to release her leg. Or so he claimed. Marina had been so grateful to be rid of the snarling, sharp-toothed barnacle that she'd indulged his delusions of psychic powers, for once.

"Hell if I know." The shadow man snorted. "Huskies are notorious escape artists. I discipline Hawk and give him plenty of exercise out of doors, but he still gets cabin fever and runs off sometimes."

"Oh." Marina frowned, nibbling at her bottom lip a little too hard and eliciting a small gasp in the process.

"Hawk won't hurt you," he hastily assured her, stepping forward. "If that's what you're afraid of."

Standing only half in shadow now, there was just enough light from the moon and the recessed lighting around the hot tub to hint at dark eyes, tawny mussed hair, sculpted facial features, and a broad muscular chest, bulging against his flannel shirt. Marina's mouth went dry. If this was an example of the area's indigenous male species, she'd come to the right place to distract herself from thoughts of Delaney.

"The name's Lucas Reynolds, by the way."

"Marina." She stepped closer to the deck railing that separated them. "Thatcher."

"This your first visit to Ogunquit, Marina Thatcher?"

The way he said her name, caressing each syllable slowly, as if he were savoring the taste of them on his tongue, caused effervescent warmth to wash over her like the hot tub's frothy swirls against her skin. "Y-yes," she croaked, trying to modulate her voice. "I live in Portland, but I've never taken the time to make the trip."

Lucas cocked his head. "So, what brings you here now?"

"A company perk, you might say."

"How long you plannin' on stayin'?" He raised an inquiring brow.

"Just for a week." Marina frowned, mirroring the sudden disappointment she felt inside.

Hawk chose that moment to dart out of the shadows, loping toward the deck as if he were going to spring up the steps. She let out a squeak and stumbled back a few steps before Lucas caught him by the collar.

"Time to go, boy." He held the straining dog. "We don't wanna scare the pretty lady before we even get a chance to know her." Hawk whined, looking very much as though he wanted to scare her. But he followed Lucas without protest as the man walked backward toward the edge of trees that bordered the yard. "My cabin's only a ten-minute walk from here." He hitched a thumb over his shoulder, indicating the path. "Feel free to drop by anytime."

"Oh, uh...thanks." Marina bit her lip, feeling suddenly shy.

"Let me know if you'll be needin' a tour guide," he called out as he disappeared through the trees.

Marina shivered. Once again she was aware that she stood there in nothing but a swimsuit and towel. Casting one last glance in the direction where Lucas had melted into the shadows, she quickly pulled the cover over the hot tub and hurried into the waiting warmth of her temporary home.

After placing a call to Reese, who obligingly agreed to drive her into town in the morning, Marina whipped up some peppermint hot chocolate and retired to her suite with the *Tarzan* book in tow.

She'd read about thirty pages when she found herself wondering what Lucas did for a living, where he'd picked up his Southern accent, and if he were as tall and handsome in broad daylight as he'd appeared in the dappled shadows of moonlight. "I guess I'll just have to find out," she muttered, tapping her index finger against her lips contemplatively.

Marina wondered if Tasha would have encouraged her to take Lucas up on his offer of a tour. Admittedly, the thought had crossed her mind. But she hadn't wanted to appear too forward. She'd only just met him, after all. Maybe there'd be time to pay him a visit after her trip into town tomorrow. Or would that be too soon? Perhaps she should wait until Saturday instead?

"Good grief!" She shook her head, a bemused smile tugging at the corners of her mouth. "I'm acting like a sixteen-year-old."

When Marina finally turned out the light and snuggled under the covers, she was still smiling. For the first time in months, she was able to fall asleep without thoughts of Foster Delaney floating through her head.

— —

On Friday morning, Reese dropped Marina off on Shore Road, near the Sparhawk Oceanfront Resort, suggesting she start her day with a leisurely stroll along the Marginal Way. The picturesque footpath apparently wound its way along the craggy promontory bordering the ocean and would lead her to Perkins Cove, the other must-see attraction the chauffeur had recommended.

The day was clear and bright, a handful of cottony clouds floating serenely across the azure canvas of sky overhead. She inhaled the salt-tinged air, lifting her face to feel the sun's kiss. Her eyes drank in the dramatic Technicolor landscape; her ears tuned to the crash of the surf against the rocky shore. All of Marina's senses came alive at once, exhilaration pulsing through her veins.

Striking out on the paved walkway, Marina strolled amid bayberry and bittersweet bushes, passing by shaded alcoves and pocket beaches. Coming to a stop in front of a high granite outcropping, her eyes feasted on the stunning views of Maine's rocky coast and the rippling blue sea beyond. She sank onto one of the many memorial benches that dotted the path, watching as people ventured out on the narrow plateau to get a better view of the crashing surf below and take pictures.

The beauty was overwhelming in its intensity and abundance. It was hard to believe she'd lived in Portland for over two years and had never made the short trip to Ogunquit until a mandatory vacation had forced her to do so. While a portion of that time had been spent caring for Tasha, most of it had been wasted as she watched life slip by from her cocoon of grief.

"Armani, no!"

Marina's attention was drawn back to the craggy ridge of rocks jutting out into the ocean. Two elegantly dressed men were attempting to snap their photograph with a cell phone, but the cat they were holding kept swiping at it. She smiled at the feline's antics and meandered over to them, extending her hand. "Here, why don't you let me take that photo for you?"

"Thanks, hon." The handsome, dark-haired man smiled appreciatively, handing her the cell phone and stepping back to stand next to the tall surfer-looking blond holding the cat.

Marina snapped several photos of the couple, but the cat continued to be uncooperative. She tried to move sideways to capture them all at an angle that caught the squirming cat looking directly into the camera, but the heel of her shoe caught in the hem of her long maxi skirt and she stumbled, unaware how close to the edge of the cliff she stood until it was too late.

Her arms flailed as she lost her balance, her body tipping backward into empty space. Her head wrenched to the side, giving her a fleeting glimpse of the jagged rocks below and the death that surely awaited her.

Time stood still. In that surreal moment, Marina thought of being reunited with her sister, reflecting on the comical scene that would occur in the afterlife when Tasha met her with an irritated *just-what-do-you think-you're-you-doing-here-already* glare.

And then she thought of Foster Delaney.

It caused a little ache in her heart to think she'd never see him again, and she wondered if he'd miss her, too. Would he spare her a fond thought from time to time? For her part, she hoped she wouldn't have to bear the burden of unrequited love throughout all eternity. Otherwise, being in heaven was going to feel an awful lot like hell.

As time snapped back to reality, Marina's purse flew from her thrashing arm. She saw the cat sail past her in a snarling blur, heard the startled gasps of spectators, and suddenly she was seized in a bruising grasp that yanked her forward, slamming her body into a rock-hard surface.

7

It took a minute for Marina to realize that the rock hard surface she'd slammed up against was the golden surfer's chest. She blinked, her lungs tried to draw in air again.

"Are you all right, sweetie?" the shorter dark-skinned man asked.

"Um, y-yeah," she wheezed, stepping out of the surfer's muscled arms. "I-I think so," she said shakily, tilting to the side.

"Whoa, there!" He righted her. His misty blue eyes narrowing with worry as they scanned over her. "You sure about that?"

"Uh huh." But she let him steady her a moment longer. "Except...I think my pride has been fatally injured." Marina cast a rueful glance at the edge of the narrow plateau. "Did either of you happen to find it smashed upon the rocks down there, because I'm pretty sure it made the dive without me."

Both men chuckled, the tall blond plucking up the cat. Armani glared balefully at Marina and bared his teeth in a hiss. The Italian-looking man handed over her purse. "I think I managed to retrieve everything that fell out of your bag, but I'm afraid this took quite a beating."

She sucked in a breath at the sight of the damaged parcel he held out, the exquisite Japanesque paper mangled on one crumpled corner. Between the excitement of meeting Lucas and Hawk the previous night, and her near-death experience just now, she'd almost forgotten about Delaney's box.

Almost.

Unfortunately, it refused to be ignored. Rather like the man himself, she grimaced. *Well, you'll just have to try harder,* she told herself sternly.

"Pardon?"

Marina startled at the voice, embarrassed to discover she'd spoken the words aloud. "Oh, uh..." She held her purse open with a casual shrug. "Just toss it in there, will you?"

"Sure, hon," he replied, carefully slipping the box into her handbag. "Now that I'm intimately acquainted with the contents of your purse, it's only proper that I introduce myself." He snickered at his joke, extending his brown hand. "James Anthony Carmichael, but my friends call me Tony."

"Marina." She shook his hand, smiling warmly. "Thatcher."

"And this"—Tony touched his companion's arm meaningfully—"is the gallant man who swooped in to rescue you before you plummeted to your death."

The golden surfer rolled his eyes. "Jake Cooper." He grinned, placing a large hand on the tabby cat's back as if he feared it might strike out at Marina. "Sorry about Armani's nasty mood. I swear he's PMSing or something."

"Believe me, I understand." Marina waved off his apology with a dismissive gesture. "My cat has chronic PMS, I think. Rarely acknowledges my existence. And when she does, she's not nice about it."

"You think they're related, Jake?" Tony snorted, slapping him on the back.

But Jake's attention was laser focused on Marina. "You sure you're OK?"

"Jake's right," Tony confirmed. "You do look a little pale."

Come to think of it, the last meal she could remember eating was dinner the night before. And she'd been so eager to explore Ogunquit this morning, the thought of breakfast hadn't really appealed to her. No wonder she was a little unsteady on her feet. As if in protest, her stomach chose that moment to gurgle loudly.

"Sounds like you could use something to eat." Jake chuckled. "We're headed down to Perkins Cove for a late lunch. Why don't you join us?"

~ ~

By the time they reached the restaurant, it was as if the three of them had been friends for ages.

Marina learned that the couple lived in the adjoining town of Wells and had been together for nearly five years. Jake worked at Wheels and Waves as a surf instructor, in addition to working at the restaurant—where they were lunching—in the off-season. Tony was a real estate agent and property manager.

Marina, in turn, had told them about her life in Portland, including her friendship with Erik and Jill, and the condo she shared with Her Majesty. When they'd inquired about her relationship status, Marina smoothly answered, "Single." But Tony had sensed her wistfulness, gently coaxing enough information from her to get the gist of her feelings for Delaney, whose name she'd discreetly withheld. It was a small world, after all, and one never knew when, or if, their acquaintances might somehow cross paths. And because Delaney was a prominent business man, she just wasn't willing to take the chance that someone in the area might know him.

After leading them to a table with a stunning ocean view, Jake disappeared with the cat and returned a few moments later with a few menus.

"Please tell me you didn't just take Armani to the kitchen," Marina joked.

"He's not on the menu...*today*." Jake snickered. "Actually, he's sort of an unofficial mascot for the restaurant. Even has his own space in the corner of the manager's office."

"Whew!" Marina blew out a mock breath of relief. "So, what do you suggest?" She gestured to the menu.

"The fried haddock," both men said in unison.

Marina scrunched up her face. "Oh dear. I, uh--"

"Don't tell me you don't like fish?" Tony arched one black brow.

"Not really." She shook her head, worrying her bottom lip with her teeth.

"Now that's adorable." Tony grinned in admiration, pointing a slender finger at her lips. "I bet you've dropped a few pairs of boxer shorts with that move!"

She felt a warm flush creep across her cheeks and hid behind her menu. Her lip biting quirk was hardly meant to make anyone lose their shorts. Half the time, she wasn't even aware she was doing it.

"Tell you what." Jake cleared his throat, and Marina thought she heard him whisper something to Tony about not embarrassing her. "Lunch is on me today," he said, lowering her menu with his large hand. "I'll get the turkey, bacon, and avocado sandwich *and* the haddock. That way, you can try both and choose the one you like best."

"You don't have to—" Marina started to protest.

A dismissive wave of Jake's hand was her only response as he headed for the kitchen to turn in their orders.

— —

"So, besides trying to get over your boss, how do you plan to spend the rest of your time here, Marina?" Tony asked.

"I'm not sure." She popped the last flaky morsel of fish into her mouth and settled back against her chair. "I'm just taking it one day at a time."

"Is it safe to assume you'll be coming back here for more haddock?" Jake flashed her an I-told-you-so grin.

"Probably," she conceded.

"What you need, Marina," Tony said, redirecting the conversation, "is some *romance*." He drew out the word, waggling his brows at her.

"You're kidding, right?" Jake retorted. "Rebound romances are the worst."

"Really?" Tony narrowed his eyes, his voice rising in pitch. "I seem to recall that *we* started out as a rebound romance."

"Oh, right." Jake choked down a mouthful of soda. "Sorry."

"You're going to have to grovel a little more than that!"

Marina covered her mouth, trying to conceal her grin as the two men bickered back and forth. A bell jingled merrily over the restaurant door, and she turned just in time to catch a glimpse of the man exiting. His dark hair was cropped short, and his tall, athletic body moved with an air of confidence and easy grace so strikingly similar to Foster Delaney that the breath caught in her lungs.

She blinked and did a double take, but the man was gone. Forcing herself to breathe normally, Marina told herself she was being ridiculous. There must be hundreds of men in the vicinity who shared physical attributes similar to those of Foster Delaney. And anyway, there was no logical reason why her employer would be in Ogunquit.

"Marina?" Tony looked at her anxiously. "Are you all right, hon?"

"Hmm?" she muttered distractedly.

Tony cast a quick glance in the direction of her gaze. "You look like you just saw a ghost."

"Maybe I did." She laughed humorlessly. "I thought I saw—" She stopped, shaking her head in disbelief.

The men leaned forward expectantly.

"My boss."

"Nuh-uh!" Tony gasped, in unison with Jake's "Whoa."

If she hadn't been so rattled by the Delaney look-alike sighting, Marina might have been amused by the comical expressions on their faces. But nothing about this felt funny. Not when she was trying to get over the very man she could have sworn she'd just seen leaving the restaurant. "I guess that sounds a tad crazy, huh?"

"Honey," Tony gave her hand a gentle squeeze, his voice echoing the sympathy in his eyes, "love makes us all a little crazy."

That's what Marina was afraid of. It hadn't even been two full days since she'd last seen Delaney, and already her tenuous resolve to forget about him during her stay in Ogunquit was teetering dangerously on a precipice of doubt caused by a figment of her imagination. She didn't know if she was hallucinating Delaney or just fantasizing about him, but either way, it was going to make it harder not to think about him now.

"Maybe you're right about the romance, Tony." Jake tapped his chin with his index finger. "Who do we know that'll do a proper job of it?"

"Actually," Marina held up a hand to forestall their speculation before they could start matchmaking in earnest. "I met someone last night."

Two pairs of eyes turned to peer at Marina.

"Do either of you happen to know Lucas Reynolds?"

"The yummy lumberjack?" Tony asked, with a little too much enthusiasm.

Marina's eyes widened. "He's a lumberjack?"

"We just call him that because he's huge. Well, that, and the fact that he wears plaid shirts and jeans all the time," Jake clarified. "Tony, here, would love to be his personal wardrobe consultant. He can't stand the idea of a fine man like that in flannel."

"I worked my magic on you, didn't I?" Tony fluttered his hand at Jake's black leather jacket and iridescent gray shirt, open at the neck to showcase an expensive-looking silver chain.

Jake kept talking as if Tony hadn't spoken. "He comes in a couple times a week for breakfast and dinner. Loves the steak here, plus we save scraps for his dog, Hawk. Lucas is kind of the quiet type. Nice guy, though."

Marina pursed her lips thoughtfully. Lucas hadn't seemed all that quiet to her last night, but maybe Jake just meant that he was private. He had been rather vague about his residency status in Ogunquit. Quiet or not, lumberjack or not, the man certainly knew how to make a flannel shirt look sexy. An image of the hunky giant in no shirt at all unconsciously flashed through her mind.

"Honey." Tony was eyeing her knowingly. "You're as red as my satin sheets. I think we'd better get you hooked up with Lucas, pronto!"

"Jeez Tony, you're embarrassing her again." Jake thumped him on the back of the head. "When do you plan to see him again, Marina?"

"Well, I was going to drop by this afternoon sometime." She cast a quick glance at the large nautical clock on the far wall. "But it's getting a little late."

"Well, don't let us stop you!" Tony started tugging at Jake's arm. "C'mon, we've got to get this girl home."

"No!" Marina blurted out, wincing when several patrons turned to stare at her. She smiled apologetically and hurried to assure Tony it wasn't necessary to leave. "I think I'll just wait until tomorrow. I didn't have anything else planned anyway."

"OK." Tony sighed disappointedly. "But you'd better call me right after you see him and let me know what happened!"

"I will," she promised, an indulgent smile tugging at the corners of her lips.

Jake rolled his eyes and glanced at the huge, orange scuba watch strapped to his wrist. "I've got to go clock in for my shift." He stood and nodded at them as he tucked his chair under the table, winking at Marina. "I'll leave you two ladies to discuss love and lumberjacks."

"Oh shoot!" She snapped her fingers as Jake disappeared into the kitchen. "I promised Erik I'd check out some possible locations for a wedding dinner—his fiancée loves it here—and I totally forgot to ask Jake if this place does special occasions."

"For your gypsy friend?" Tony inquired.

"Erik, yes."

"Why don't you let me take care of that for you?" he offered eagerly, practically bouncing in his chair. "I also know the other area venues really well, and I have a lot of connections through my job."

"It's nice of you to offer," Marina said appreciatively. "But I'd hate to put you through the trouble for someone you don't even know."

"Nonsense," Tony clucked, waving away her concern with a dismissive gesture. "I'm hopelessly impassioned by anything that has to do with romance, whether I'm planning for a wedding or closing on a house."

"What?" She gaped at him. "You think real estate is romantic?"

"It can be, yes," he said resolutely.

"I don't see how." Marina wrinkled her nose. "But I'll buy you dinner sometime, if you can convince me."

A huge grin split across Tony's face. "You are *soooo* going to lose your wallet on this one, hon." Leaning his forearms on the table, he clasped his hands together. "About five or six months ago, I helped this guy buy a cabin for a woman he cares for very deeply."

"Well, that's really sweet but—"

Tony held up a hand to cut her off. "Here's the romantic part..." He paused dramatically for effect. "He hasn't told the woman how he feels yet."

"What?" Marina snorted in disbelief. "But what if she doesn't return his affections? He'll have wasted all that money for nothing!"

"Actually, it's a really good investment." Tony pointed out. "But yes, you're right. It's a huge emotional risk. And that's exactly what makes it such an epic romantic gesture. He's putting everything on the line and hoping she'll return his feelings."

"He must really love her," she murmured, wondering what it would be like to have someone love *her* that much. There had been moments when she'd thought Foster Delaney might actually care for her the way she did for him. There'd been something about the way he'd looked at her that day in the park, something in the way he'd stared at her lips that night at the pub. And what about the dance they'd shared at the company work party? Had she only imagined the energy that had snapped and pinged between them like hot sparks of electricity? She must have, Marina reasoned. She was most likely transposing her own hopes and desires onto the reactions she wanted most to see from Delaney.

Tony gave her hand a gentle squeeze. "You're thinking of *him*, aren't you?"

"I can't seem to stop myself." She choked out a bitter laugh.

"Have you ever considered telling him how you feel?" He studied her thoughtfully. "You know, making your own grand romantic gesture?"

"Not going to happen, Tony."

"Why not?" He thrust out his palms. "What do you have to lose?"

"You mean, besides my job?" she questioned incredulously. Holding up a hand, she started ticking off more reasons on her fingers. "Let's see—my pride, my principles, my—"

"OK, I get the picture." Tony pursed his lips. "But, honey, if you think he's emotionally unavailable and physically off limits, why are you wasting your energy on him?"

It was a valid question. One her head totally agreed with. Unfortunately, her heart was much harder to convince.

8

Marina lounged on the sofa in the great room. Orange fingers of flame crackled in the fireplace, the warmth embracing her like a cozy blanket as she listened to the heavy rain drum against the aluminum roof.

Setting aside the *Tarzan* book she'd been reading, her mind lazily reflected upon the day's events. She marveled at her fortune in having encountered Tony and Jake. Almost unconsciously, she'd found herself unburdening her pent-up emotions upon them until she'd spilled every last detail of Tasha's illness, her breakup with Grayson, and her increasing affection for her employer.

Marina shook her head, a wry smile tugging at the corners of her mouth. Tony should have been a therapist. She wondered if the poor fool who'd purchased the cabin for his ladylove had felt a similar compulsion to divulge his whole life story to Tony as well.

After lunch, she and Tony had wandered through the boutiques in Perkins Cove, ending up at the Ogunquit Museum of American Art. Marina hadn't paid much attention to the art collections, but the gardens and views of the coast had enthralled her. While they waited outside the museum for Reese to arrive, Tony had asked her about the gift box in her purse.

"Was it a gift from your employer, Delaney?"

Her lips parted in surprise. "How did you know?"

"There was something about the way you looked at it." His tone softened. "I saw all these emotions reflected in your expression—confusion, wonder, anxiety, longing, sadness, and hope—the same emotions I saw on your face when you told Jake and me about him."

Marina sighed. "Maybe I'm making a big deal out of the whole thing. But I feel like, I don't know..." She shook her head. "Like if I open that box, I'm inviting inappropriate involvement."

"Why?" Tony's dark brows slanted into a frown. "Has your employer asked you out or made inappropriate advances toward you?"

"Well, no."

"Then I don't see a problem," he assured her, though he seemed disappointed by her admission. "Look, sweetie, employers give their employees gifts all the time. Besides, what's in that box could be as innocuous as a paper weight." He leaned toward her with a conspiratorial wink. "But you won't know that unless you open it."

Marina drew her lips in thoughtfully. Tony was right. She was probably making a big deal out of nothing and causing herself unnecessary misery in the process. Tonight she'd open Delaney's gift and find out whether or not she actually had something to worry about. "Thanks for the advice."

"Anytime, hon." He programmed his cell phone number into her own, admonishing her that she was to call him at any hour of the day or night if she needed anything at all. Tossing a business card in her purse, he embraced her in a big bear hug and said he'd call when he finalized his ideas for wedding venues. He'd also made her promise to keep him updated on any new developments with Lucas.

Marina smiled at the memory. She felt certain theirs was a friendship that would last beyond her brief stay in Ogunquit. Already, she was planning to invite Tony and Jake to visit her in Portland.

Yawning, she let her head sag against the back of the sofa, her cheek pressing against the couch's soft surface. The smell of the leather made her think of woods, with traces of citrus and mint. She scoffed at the direction her thoughts had taken. It seemed everything was hell-bent on reminding her of Delaney on this trip, from the sofa's unique aroma to the man she'd glimpsed leaving the restaurant.

Her eyes shifted over to the coffee table where Delaney's box had been neglected since she'd returned from town. Her hands shook as she reached for the box. Peeling away the torn wrapping paper, she nudged off the lid.

Marina's eyes widened, an audible gasp escaping her parted lips.

Gently prying the jade dolphin figurine from its snug-fitting foam encasement, Marina turned it over in her hands, inspecting it for damage. Fortunately, the box's dense packing had done its job admirably when the unopened parcel had tumbled from her purse earlier.

Transfixed, she traced her fingers over the smooth, stone sculpture. The jade was expertly carved to depict, in stunning detail, a dolphin jumping from the sea, perched atop the crest of a wave. The luster of the polished stone mimicked the sheen of a dolphin's wet skin, giving it a lifelike quality.

"It's beautiful," she whispered, her attention suddenly drawn to a small flap of paper tucked inside the upturned box lid. Pulling it loose, she unfolded it with trembling fingers.

I saw this at a little shop in Japan and thought of you. ~ F. D.

Marina read the note again, and then once more, scarce able to believe Delaney was aware of such an insignificant detail as her obsession with dolphins. It made his gift all the more intimate, and she feared it would weaken her dwindling ability to remain impartial to the man. Already, the tender feelings his gift had invoked were causing pangs of longing in her chest. Closing her eyes, she did some yoga breathing to restore her sense of balance.

As long as Delaney is your employer, she reminded herself, *it would be unwise to let your heart run away with your head.*

Still, she couldn't keep herself from speculating on the nature of Delaney's gift. Was it a friendly gesture or romantic one? Shaking her head at her foolishness, Marina yawned again and considered taking herself up to bed. But she was as reluctant to leave the comfort of the sofa as it was to release its hold on her.

And besides, it would be a shame to waste a perfectly good fire by not falling asleep in front of it. Gently setting the jade dolphin on the coffee table, she snuggled into the couch and let the low murmur of rain lull her into the welcome oblivion of sleep.

Unfortunately, Delaney followed her there, too.

— —

Jolting awake, Marina glanced at her surroundings in confusion as consciousness slowly returned. With an exasperated breath, she sagged back against the sofa.

She'd dreamed of Delaney again.

In truth, other than last night, the man hadn't really left her alone since she'd arrived in Ogunquit. First, she'd deliberately left Delaney's gift in the limo yesterday only to have Reese dutifully retrieve it for her. Then Tony had gone and rescued the blasted thing after she took that nasty tumble, and they'd spent the afternoon discussing the very man who'd given it to her. But worst of all, her imagination had conjured an apparition of her employer at the restaurant where they'd dined in Perkins Cove. It was enough to make her wonder if Foster Delaney would haunt her in some form or another wherever she went.

She seriously needed a distraction from her thoughts.

Perhaps a bracing dose of Maine's brisk night air would do the trick? Tilting her head, she listened for rain, but as near as she could tell, the storm had abated. Rising from the sofa, Marina lazily stretched her limbs. As she was about to slip her feet into her shoes, images of Hawk bursting out of the dark forest, eyes glowing hungrily, made her plop back down on the couch again.

She knew she was being insanely ridiculous. The animal probably wasn't nearly as threatening as her imagination made him out to be.

Besides, Lucas had assured her that Hawk wouldn't hurt her. But her irrational fear extinguished her desire for fresh air. "Honestly," she scolded herself, "dwelling on your absurd paranoia of dogs is about as useless as wishing Delaney's gift actually means something special—"

Her thoughts skidded to a halt at the sound of deck planks groaning under the weight of heavy foot falls.

Someone was on the front porch.

Marina's hand flew to her mouth before the squeak of panic tickling her throat could escape. Her gaze darted to the antique wall clock. Ten twenty-three. Who would be paying a visit at this hour? She didn't remember seeing any signs of neighbors in the immediate vicinity, and the only people who knew she was staying at this particular residence were Lucas, Reese, and...

Delaney.

Why did all her waking thoughts seem to lead back to her employer, even at the most inopportune times? Shaking her head, she whipped her attention back to the problem at hand. There was a prowler outside. What did he want? Was she in danger?

Her eyes flew to the front door. As tired as she was, she'd forgotten to lock up for the night. Whoever was outside simply had to twist the door knob to gain entrance into the cabin.

Bolting from the couch, she snatched the fire poker from its stand on the hearth. Heaven help her if she actually had to use it as a weapon. Her hand was shaking so badly, she doubted she could inflict much damage on an assailant if called upon to protect herself. No, she'd be better off if she could throw the deadbolt on the door before the intruder decided to invite himself in.

As Marina lurched forward, one of her feet hooked under the rug and the other caught on the leg of an end table, toppling her forward. The metal poker hit the hardwood floor with a loud clatter. And she followed it, her abdomen and head striking the wood floor with a hard smack.

She heard the door crash open, and then a black void of unconsciousness claimed her.

Marina floated in a gray haze of pain and bewilderment. Her stomach felt a little queasy, and when she tried to shift her position on the bed, she gasped at the sharp pain that shot through the right side of her ribcage.

The bed dipped beside her as gentle hands pushed her back against the pillows and placed something freezing cold on her forehead. "Take it easy, Marina."

She turned in the direction of the soothing male voice, her eyes straining against the stars obstructing her vision. The shadow of familiarity that clung to the voice was quickly absorbed by the fog clouding her brain. "Who's there?"

"It's Foster. Delaney."

"Delaney?" Shadowy images drifted through her thoughts. Had she only dreamed being cradled against the warmth of a firm chest, of strong arms gently placing her upon her bed? Had she imagined the soft lips that pressed a kiss to her forehead and the winter-fresh breath that caressed her skin? "I-I think I dreamed about you." She frowned. Why was she so confused?

A short silence preceded the man's response. "Did you?"

"I-I don't know," Marina muttered dazedly. "Everything's so... fuzzy." She raised a shaky hand to her cold head, her fingers dislodging the ice pack.

"Well, things will be clearer after you get some rest." The man plucked away the ice pack as it slid into the crook of her neck, the simple brush of his fingers against her skin causing her to shiver anew. "I'll be nearby, if you need me."

She knew the instant he was gone and felt oddly bereft, though she couldn't say why. Her head was pounding too hard to think rationally, so she gave into her fatigue and sank back into a black numbness.

When she woke up several hours later, it was still dark. Silvery moonlight filtered through the sunburst window above, highlighting a room that looked foreign to her adjusting eyes. She jolted to a sitting position and was rewarded with a sharp jab to her side and a dizzying stab of pain to her head.

Placing palms to her temples, she struggled to piece together the jumble of memories swimming in her head. If she was remembering things correctly, she was not in her condo in Portland. Dim recollections of arriving at an insanely large and luxurious cabin by way of a limo, of striking ocean views, and of enjoying lunch with friends, niggled at the back of her mind.

But the nebulous memories that unsettled her most were of a door crashing open, of being carried to bed and hearing a man's voice whispering to her in the darkness. Marina remembered the soothing timbre of his voice, the gentle pressure of his hand pushing her back against the bed.

What had he said his name was? Why was he here? While she didn't recall feeling threatened by him, it bothered her that she didn't know who he was. Or did she? Regardless, in her current state of physical distress, with her memory fractured and her body bruised, the stranger was all she had.

And she needed answers.

—◆—

"Mister?" Marina called out in a strained voice. "Mister?" she cried out again.

She heard a scuffle, a low-muttered curse, and then the man was there again, pulling her into the shelter of his arms. "Shhh, I'm here." He held her close against him, yet delicately, as if she were a fine piece of china.

Marina's first instinct was to resist him. He was a stranger. She should be fighting the uncontrollable urge to melt against the tempting warmth of his chest. But it felt so amazing being cocooned in the masculine strength of his embrace.

"W-what's wrong with me?" she asked in a shaky voice, pressing her face into the crook of his neck. He smelled incredible, like woods, and man, with a whisper of citrus and mint. She reveled in the feel of his solid frame, real and tangible, unlike the mindless fog and shadowy hallucinations she'd been floating in for what seemed like whole days and only minutes at the same time. How long had it actually been?

"From what the doctor could ascertain over the phone, you've bruised your ribs." He drew back to study her face, concern etched in his features. "I'm not hurting you, am I?"

She shook her head, wishing he would pull her back into his embrace. He didn't.

"He also suspects that you may have sustained a concussion as well." Gently setting her away from him, he flipped on the light switch near the bed and Marina winced at the flood of light. "Sorry," he grimaced sympathetically. "You don't have an urge to vomit, do you?"

"Not anymore." The twinge of queasiness she'd felt when she'd woken up the first time had quickly passed.

"Good." He nodded. "I'll be checking on you throughout the night. I need to make sure your confusion isn't worsening and that you can be roused from sleep."

As her vision slowly adjusted to the shock of light, Marina admired the handsome face before her. His short-cropped hair was a deep, rich brown, the color of roasted coffee beans. The barest hint of stubble darkened his jaw, and his green eyes glittered like jewels. Those eyes held a vague familiarity that intrigued her, holding her captive, until the spell ruptured with a flash of blinding pain. She sucked in a sharp breath, her hand moving to the swollen lump above her right eyebrow.

"Easy, that's quite a knot you've got there." The man leaned forward, lifting her hand away from the bruised flesh on her head. As he did, the enticingly masculine scent she'd smelled on him only moments ago drifted to her nostrils.

Marina tilted her head. Why did that fragrant blend of woods, citrus, and mint seem so familiar? And then it was as if a rusty key turned a lock in her head, releasing one of its reluctant secrets. "D-Delaney?"

"Yes, good." He expelled an audible breath. "I'm relieved your memory is improving."

Marina pursed her lips. Well, not all of it, apparently. There were chinks in the mortar of her memory that still needed to be filled in. But at least one mystery had been solved. Delaney must have been her late-night visitor, the one she'd heard on the porch earlier. The same person who'd crashed through the cabin door. And the soothing voice she'd heard as she first surfaced from unconsciousness.

But none of that explained *why* he was here. Marina scrunched up her face, a riot of confusing questions flitting through her head. Had Erik's gypsy intuition warned him she was in some sort of trouble? Had he convinced Delaney to come check on her? If Erik had felt something were wrong, why hadn't he come himself? For that matter, if she remembered Erik, why couldn't she recall Delaney's reason for being here? *Ugh!* She bit back a scream of frustration as she tried to fight her way through the cobwebs strangling her logic. In her opinion, being concussed ranked right up there with dog attacks.

Dog attacks?

Marina blanched at the thought. Frantically, she pushed aside the bed covers, ignoring the twinge of pain in her ribs. Yanking up her pant legs, she turned her legs this way and that, searching for bruises where canine teeth might have broken the surface.

Abruptly, strong hands curled around her upper arms to still her. "Marina, Marina!" Delaney's anxious voice wrenched her from her fruitless task. "What's wrong?"

She blinked, the frown creasing her forehead pulling uncomfortably at the tender lump above her brow. "W-was I bitten by a dog?"

"I guess your memories will require a little more time to sort themselves out." A small half smile tugged at Delaney's lips. "You did have a little run-in with a dog, back in April, I believe."

"Oh." Marina caught her bottom lip between her teeth. Well, at least she hadn't imagined it. She supposed a full recollection of the unpleasant event would return eventually, along with the rest of her memories. She just hoped it wouldn't take too long, because she couldn't shake the niggling feeling that Delaney's presence at the cabin was fundamentally wrong somehow.

She was suddenly very aware of the feel of Delaney's hands where they lingered on her upper arms, an enticingly warm sensation at odds with the tendril of uneasiness snaking through her. Shrugging out of his grasp, Marina settled back against the pillows to put as much distance between them as possible.

"Can I get you anything?" Delaney gestured to her bed covers. "Are you warm enough? Do you need more blankets? What about painkillers? The doctor said you could take Tylenol or ibuprofen—"

"No," she cut him off. "I think I'd just like to be alone. I'm confused, and I-I don't really feel comfortable with you here right now."

"All right." He sighed, his lips tugging down at the corners. Rubbing the back of his neck, he stood and crossed the room, stopping at the door. "But call for me, if you need anything, OK?"

"The only thing I need," she muttered as he disappeared from view, "is my memory back."

9

*M*arina was having the most incredible dream.

She lay cradled in Foster Delaney's warm embrace, his muscled arm draped possessively across her abdomen. He pulled her back against his chest, spooning her body under the bedcovers. Yawning contentedly, she turned to face him.

His mouth hung open slightly, a soft snore vibrating through his lips. In sleep, his face betrayed a man younger than his thirty-six years. She liked how the stubble darkening his jaw gave his features an edgy appearance quite at odds with his usual CEO-polished countenance. His pillow-mussed hair demanded her touch, and her fingers slipped through the tousled mess of spiky, brown tufts of their own volition. Delaney sighed and stirred in his sleep, the movement evincing provocative notes of citrus, mint, and woods that tickled her nose.

Marina withdrew her hand, rubbing at the frown pinching her brows together. A vague recollection of Delaney insisting she take a vacation pricked at the periphery of her mind, followed by the memory of her arrival at the luxury cabin he'd rented, and another of Delaney holding her in his arms sometime during the night.

Or had she only dreamed all that, just as she was dreaming of Foster Delaney in bed with her now? As if in answer to her unspoken thoughts, the man in question tightened his hold around her waist. A shiver of awareness rippled through her body. And that's when Marina knew.

She. Was. Not. Dreaming.

Her eyes widened, a squeak of anxiety escaping her gaping mouth as another, more disturbing, thought presented itself. Had she and Delaney been intimate? Had they done something they'd both regret when they returned to work?

Marina scrambled from the bed, hissing at the sharp twinge of pain in her ribs. Grabbing her pillow, and wincing with the effort, Marina gave Delaney a few satisfying thwacks.

"Wake. Up!"

"W-what's wrong?" Delaney sat up groggily. The bewilderment in his emerald gaze quickly cleared, honing in on Marina. "What is it?" he asked.

"For starters," she snapped, pointing an accusing finger at him, "you're in my bed!"

"Oh, that." Delaney stretched languidly, unperturbed, just as Her Majesty often did when caught slumbering where she ought not. He yawned, scratching his head. "I guess I must've fallen asleep in here the last time I checked on you."

"Oh." So they hadn't been intimate. Of course not. Some deep-rooted feminine instinct told her she would've remembered *that*. What she did recall, quite vividly all of a sudden, was the image of being pressed against Delaney's muscled chest, his fingers gliding soothingly over her back as she whimpered in the dark. As much as she'd wanted her memory back, some things were best left forgotten because, if Marina was remembering it accurately, she'd enjoyed the experience far too much for her own good.

Pursing her lips, she shoved the memory aside, struggling to hold on to her indignation. "Would you mind telling me what you're doing here, Delaney?"

He ignored her question. "Foster, if you don't mind."

"I do." She replied stiffly, repeating herself. "Why are you here?"

"I told you." He cocked his head, his forehead creasing in mock confusion. "I fell asleep in here when I came to check on you."

"You know what I mean."

"Okay, look. I know I owe you an explanation." He ran a hand through his hair. "But can't it wait until after breakfast? I'm starving."

Marina could barely control the urge to roll her eyes at him. She knew what he was up to. He wasn't the first man of her acquaintance who cried hunger when he wished to change the subject.

"You must be hungry, too." Delaney amended when she continued to glare at him. "You haven't eaten anything since I arrived last night, and it's after eleven now."

"I was a little...preoccupied."

"Yeah, concussions will do that to you." He flashed her a sympathetic grin, twin divots peeking out from his whiskered cheeks.

Marina flushed under the assault of Delaney's dimples. But she wasn't about to let him off the hook, especially after his odd behavior over the past week. "Did you flip a personality switch since you left the office?" She regarded him through narrowed eyes. "Because, you're acting so—"

Delaney held up his hand to cut her off. "I know, I know. And I promise to explain everything." He slid off the bed and shuffled through the door without looking back at her or waiting for a response. "*After* we eat."

"Fine." Marina huffed, scowling at his retreating form. It was only then she realized that he was wearing street clothes. Had he slept like that all night long? She gnawed on her bottom lip, guilt prickling at her conscience.

She'd just railed at the man who'd given up his own comfort all night to see to hers.

—◆ ◆—

When Marina emerged from the bathroom half an hour later, she assumed that the hot shower she'd enjoyed would help her look and feel more refreshed.

Well, she did feel better. But the image that greeted her in the full-length bedroom mirror was disappointing. The blue eyes staring back at her were ringed with dark, purplish shadows, and her customary peaches-and-cream complexion was sallow, even under a careful application of makeup. The swollen lump on her head had gone down slightly, and she'd managed to cover the bruised flesh with concealer and some strategic hair parting.

Her face might have taken a toll from her injury and fitful night's sleep, but at least her raven-colored hair was no worse for wear, hanging sleek and shiny over her shoulders like a smooth, black waterfall.

She'd dressed in what she considered her power outfit, a white silk blouse and pair of tailored black slacks. Shivering, she realized her feet were still bare, but the thought of having to bend over to pull on a pair of socks and shoes made her wince. A quick scan of the bedroom did not turn up the shoes she'd worn yesterday. Had she left them downstairs? Marina eyed the shoe choices left to her: a pair of boots, and the fluffy blue doggy slippers she'd packed on a whim. She doubted Delaney would take her seriously in a pair of overstuffed novelty slippers, but at this point, it was a risk she was willing to take for the sake of warmth and comfort.

Peering down at her feet, Marina had to admit that the slippers looked ridiculous. She smiled at the memory of how her royal-pain-in-the-butt cat, Her Majesty, had immediately taken exception to the inanimate puffy pooches, snarling and scratching at her feet whenever Marina wore them. When she'd packed them to wear around the cabin, she never imagined that anyone but herself would actually see them.

Still, Marina was glad she'd brought the slippers with her. As one of the last gifts Tasha had given her before she passed away, they held a special place in her heart. Having them near made her feel, in some small way, that Tasha was with her, too. And she could use a little sisterly support right now.

"Well, guys," she said, wiggling her cartoony-canine feet, "let's go find out what the devil Foster Delaney is doing here—and get rid of him—so we can all get on with our lives."

By the time Marina managed the walk from her bedroom to the second-floor landing, her impatience to deal with Foster Delaney deteriorated about as fast as the delicious aromas wafting up the stairs reached her traitorous nostrils.

Her stomach rumbled as she inhaled the fragrant notes of brewing coffee, sizzling bacon, and browning French toast, reminding her that she hadn't eaten anything since Friday afternoon. That thought was quickly replaced by another. How on earth was she supposed to sit across from her employer over breakfast and small talk under such awkward circumstances? When her stomach growled again by the time she'd reached the bottom of the stairs, Marina decided the breakfast that awaited her was worth a little awkwardness.

Leaning against the cabinets, she watched Delaney navigate his way around the large kitchen as if he belonged there. He'd showered and changed into an ivory-colored, cable-knit sweater that hugged his athletic form, along with a pair of snug-fitting jeans that stirred an appetite that had little to do with French toast, bacon, and coffee.

Blast his gorgeous hide.

She tugged her eyes away from the enticing view of his well-built physique to study the table to her left, set with square-cut black plates and decorative black-and-white ceramic mugs. Her eyes narrowed as they lit upon the flower arrangement in the center of the table that hadn't been there the day before. A stylish black vase complemented a mixture of ivory roses and cheerful white daisies with sunny yellow centers. Her favorite.

Before she had time to contemplate what that meant, Delaney was turning to greet her, twin plates piled high with steaming bacon and French toast perched in his hands. "I thought I heard you come in. Are you ready for the best French toast you've ever—" The question died on his lips as his eyes dropped to her feet, a bemused smile tugging at the corners of his sexy mouth and releasing the full force of his dimples.

She wanted to wipe the smirk off his face, but with those dimples winking at her, it was hard to form a rational response. "I-I, uh, couldn't find my other shoes and my feet were cold." She shrugged, shuffling over to the table to sink gingerly into a chair.

"Your shoes are over there by the couch." Delaney flicked his chin in the direction of the great room, unloading his burdens on the table before heading back to the counter to collect the coffeepot. "I see you got my gift." He cast her a sidelong glance over his shoulder.

Marina's eyes widened as the memory of it slammed home. In the aftermath of last night's injury, she'd completely forgotten about the jade dolphin Delaney had given her. But now that she recalled how deeply his gift had touched her and how the gesture had caused her to question Delaney's intentions, she felt ill-prepared to deal with it in her present condition.

"Oh, uh...yes, thank you." Though his expression remained impassive as he lowered himself into the chair across from her, the slight tick of his jaw convinced Marina that her response had been inadequate.

"It's exquisite," she amended her reply. "It must have been very expensive."

Delaney's face brightened as he waved off her concern. "The cost was of little consequence. Besides, it made me happy to buy it for you."

His words caused her heart to flutter, and she wasn't sure how to reply to that. In the end, she decided on something safe and neutral. "Thank you."

"You're very welcome." He offered her a dimpled smile and poured her a cup of coffee. "I noticed you're reading *Tarzan*?"

"Yes." Marina sighed in relief, grateful for Delaney's change of subject. "It's one of my favorite books."

"Mine, too." Delaney gestured for her to begin eating. "I'm surprised. Not many people know what a literary treasure it is. I was lucky enough to have a father who read me the entire series when I was just a kid."

Marina tried to imagine a young Foster Delaney listening in rapt attention as his father read to him from the jungle tales of *Tarzan of the Apes*. In her mind's eye, his wide green eyes glittered with anticipation, his mop of longish brown hair repeatedly falling into his sun-kissed face as his little body bobbed up and down with excitement. She felt a rush of tenderness for the little boy of her imagination and wondered how closely she'd captured the likeness of his youth.

"Mind telling me what you're smiling about?"

"What?" She startled back to the present at the amusement in his voice. "Oh. I, uh...was just thinking how delicious this French toast is."

For the next twenty minutes, Marina tried to convince Delaney—and herself—that breakfast, and other benign subjects, were the *only* thing on her mind.

10

"Will you let me take you somewhere?" Delaney asked when they'd finished eating.

Marina looked at him askance. "I thought you were going to explain why you're here in Ogunquit?"

"I will. I promise." He reached out as if to place his hand over hers, but then he pulled his arm back and rested it in front of him instead. "But there's something I'd really like to show you first, if you feel up to it." His fingers traced a lazy rhythm along the table's surface as he waited for her to reply. Marina followed the pattern of his fingers with her eyes, wondering what it would feel like if his fingers were to glide across her skin like that. She felt heat creep up her neck and quickly banished the thought from her mind.

"You won't have to walk," Delaney rushed to assure her. "I can drive you there in the golf cart. It takes about fifteen minutes or so to get there, but it's an easy ride, and it's beautiful out, and I'm sure you'll love it..."

He was rambling.

Marina thought it was adorable. But then she started to wonder if he was just trying to come up with clever ways to avoid "the talk." Then she decided she didn't care. As much as her body was hurting, the thought of lounging around the house all day didn't thrill her. Besides, her eyes shifted to the open window. Delaney was right. It *was* beautiful out. What would it hurt to take a little field trip?

"All right," she agreed. "I'll need my shoes and a sweat—"

Before she could finish, Delaney was out of his chair. He returned a moment later with her shoes in one hand and the lap blanket from the sofa in the other. Kneeling down in front of her, he gently removed her doggy slippers, one at a time, and set them aside. Slowly, he lifted one foot to slide on her shoe, and then the other. Delaney's touch made her skin prickle with sensation.

He must've mistaken her shudders for a chill, because his head snapped up, his brows furrowing, as he quickly pulled the lap blanket around her shoulders. "Wait here and I'll pull the golf cart around to the front door. It's an easier walk than taking you through the garage."

When she heard the door to the garage close, Marina blew out her pent-up breath. She didn't know how much longer she could pretend that Delaney's presence didn't tear her up inside.

＞　＜

"What is this place?" Marina glanced around in awe as they entered the golden-hued clearing.

Tree boughs arched into a protective canopy overhead, the sun shining through the veil of yellow, scarlet, and orange leaves like stained glass windows in a domed arboreal cathedral. In the center of the clearing was a flat area, in a circular shape, encircled by a mound of earth. Crudely built stone benches were nestled around the periphery of the man-made earthwork. She could only describe the atmosphere in the grove as otherworldly, a place where one could imagine secret faerie rituals being performed within the depression of the mound.

"Some say it was an ancient druidic worshiping place." Delaney helped her to one of the stone benches. "But it's more likely the work of the Native American tribes who once occupied these lands." He sat down beside her on the narrow stone slab, his shoulders and thighs touching hers.

"How did you find it?" Marina asked, desperately trying to distract herself from his nearness.

He leaned forward, resting his forearms on his thighs. "I spent some time in Ogunquit after my wife died, and I took a lot of long, contemplative walks. One day, I came across a tree, not far from the cabin, with a symbol carved into it." He stood and crossed over to a nearby pine, pointing out the hieroglyphic-looking mark that scarred the tree's flesh.

"I followed the marks and ended up here." He spread his arms in a wide arc and let out a sigh. "I can't explain it, but I felt like I was supposed to find this place."

Marina didn't say anything. She sensed that Delaney was lost in his own thoughts, and she didn't want to end this rare glimpse into his personal life.

"There's almost something, I don't know..." He shook his head and shrugged. "Mystical about it. Healing, even."

She tilted her head, a small smile tugging at one corner of her mouth. "You don't strike me as the type to believe in magic."

"No." He grimaced, stuffing his hands into the pockets of his jeans. "Not since my wife died."

"But this place"—Marina gestured at their surroundings—"changed your mind?"

The expression on his face turned brooding, closed off, and unreadable, mirroring the one from the office on Wednesday morning, when she'd looked up to find his gaze fixed upon her.

"We should get you back to the cabin now," he said gruffly.

— ~

Foster Delaney paced the floor in front of the stone fireplace.

If he were any other man, Marina might think he were nervous. But when Delaney paced, it generally meant he was deep in contemplation.

Or stalling.

She voted for stalling. He seemed in no hurry to divulge his reasons for coming to Ogunquit, which he'd promised to do after showing her the clearing. Since returning from their drive, however, he'd been quiet and withdrawn. Marina had been taken aback by his sudden change of mood in the clearing and had been relieved to leave the place behind, along with the personal connection they'd shared there. One more experience like that and she might lose her heart to him completely. It hadn't helped that the atmosphere in the clearing had been charged with an ethereal quality that made it difficult to be levelheaded.

When they'd returned to the cabin, Delaney had busied himself cleaning up their breakfast dishes—another stalling tactic?—while Marina rested on the couch. After he'd tidied the kitchen, he'd joined her in the great room where he now treaded back and forth across the length of the Ikat-print rug before the hearth. She chewed at her bottom lip, wondering what was troubling him.

The thought made her stomach do a weird little flip-flop. Had Foster Delaney discovered her feelings for him? If so, what were his intentions? If he simply wanted to remind her that their relationship was strictly professional, he could have done that easily enough at the office. No, she feared there was more to it than that.

Well, crap.

"What did you say?" Delaney had stopped pacing, his eyes narrowing as he studied her face. "Are you sure you're up to this?"

Good grief. She really needed to stop voicing her thoughts. "Yes," she reassured him, shifting her position on the couch. "I'm good."

"Well, I'm not." Ducking around the sofa, he made a beeline the kitchen. "I think I need a drink."

"You've been trying to avoid this conversation since I found you in my bed this morning," Marina reminded him. It was absurd that the man famous for closing multi-million dollar business deals couldn't manage a simple conversation with his employee. Gingerly she stood up and turned just in time to see him pull a bottle of Scotch from a low cabinet near the dining table. "Just come out with it already!"

"I will, I will." He poured a dash of the amber liquid into a glass tumbler. "I just need a little help getting started." He downed the Scotch with a grimace.

Marina had never known Delaney to drink much alcohol. It was just one more inconsistency in his recent behavior that made her question whether she really knew the man at all. Uncertainty and impatience twisted at her gut. "Delaney..." she pleaded.

He didn't bother to correct her use of his surname this time. Leaning against the kitchen cabinet, he scrubbed a hand over his face. "I guess you've probably noticed that I haven't been myself lately."

His green eyes blazed like glittering emerald fires, and Marina felt herself being sucked into them, her lungs siphoned of air. But his next words snapped her from the captivating effect of his gaze.

"You know it's because of *you*, right?"

She felt the blood drain from her face in a dizzying flush. *He knew.* She was at once embarrassed and ashamed that her employer was aware of her feelings and not a little apprehensive about what it meant for her career, and her heart. Marina tried to convince herself that she should be grateful Delaney knew the truth. Trying to conceal her feelings for him over the past four and a half months had been pure hell. Now, she'd have no choice but to confront it and move on.

She should be relieved. But she wasn't. She loved her job at Argyle, and it grieved her to think she might be only seconds away from losing it.

"You don't look so hot." Delaney straightened away from the kitchen cabinet and stepped toward her. "Maybe we should finish this conversation later."

Marina's hand flew up to stop his approach. "No, I'd like to finish up the details of my dismissal right now, if you don't mind."

A grim frown settled over his features. "Dismissal?"

"Isn't that what all of this is about?" She swept her arms out on either side of her, indicating the cabin's spacious interior. She didn't know why the idea hadn't occurred to her before. "A consolation prize, of sorts, for losing my job?"

Delaney cocked his head, his dark brows climbing to his hairline. "You think I'm here to fire you?"

"Aren't you?" Marina asked incredulously.

"Not hardly." He let out a harsh bark of laughter, rubbing at the back of his neck. "I'm here for a different reason entirely."

Doubt and confusion skittered through her. Only a moment ago she'd been so certain of Delaney's reason for being in Ogunquit. But now she was back to the niggling anxiety she'd experienced when she'd first become aware that something felt amiss about his presence at the cabin. Marina eyed him warily. "And what would that be?"

Delaney didn't respond. He simply stood there, his gaze smoldering with the intensity of indefinable emotions. She'd seen that expression once before, that night at the pub, when they'd been waiting outside for Erik. Or had she only imagined it? Regardless, she could no longer bear the heavy weight of his silent brooding.

"Tell me why you're here."

Too late, Marina realized her words had provoked something dangerous and feral in her employer. In a blur of motion, he closed the distance between them, his arms braced against the cabinet behind her, hemming her in on either side. "I'm. Here," he rasped out, enunciating each word deliberately. "For. *You.*"

His closeness sent her pulse racing. If he leaned any closer, his lips would touch hers. Marina shrank back against the cabinet to put as much distance between them as possible, throwing up a mental shield to block the image of kissing Delaney. Nothing, she reminded herself sternly, could happen between them as long as he was her employer. She needed to reign in her body's chaotic reactions and ease the tension crackling between them if she was going to come through this thing with her heart, and her dignity, intact.

Tilting up her chin defiantly, Marina tried to control her trembling voice. "I don't know what you mean."

Delaney abruptly shoved away from her, muttering a low curse. "Oh, come on, Marina." He rubbed at the bridge of his nose. "You're an intelligent woman. I'm sure you can figure it out."

Anger speared through her as the implication of what he was saying sunk in. "So...what, you're here for an illicit office fling?" Something about the way he stood there, his heated green gaze boring into her, confirmed her suspicion. All the pieces were clicking into place in her mind...Erik's insistence that Delaney was totally infatuated with her. The "forced" vacation, arranged by Delaney himself. The extravagant accommodations paid by her employer. The remote location. Delaney's unexpected appearance at the cabin.

Another woman might feel flattered by such overtures from a man like Delaney, but Marina felt only a sickening thud of betrayal and disappointment in her stomach.

"I won't deny that I want to make love to you." Delaney's slow, seductive gaze slid downward, to her lips, her neck. Stepping closer, he slid a hand beneath her hair to gently cup the column of her throat, his thumb caressing her jaw.

Marina found herself leaning into Delaney's caress, her eyes fluttering closed. Desire crested through her, roaring loudly in her ears like ocean waves crashing against Maine's rugged coastline. She wanted to feel Delaney's hands on her body, his skin next to hers, their bodies intimately joined.

But she wanted those things for a lifetime, not one night, or a succession of nights, as his mistress. She deserved more than that. It was galling to think that Delaney had such a low opinion of her personal worth.

Indignation flared bright and hot within her, igniting her overwrought nerves. Catching them both unaware, Marina's hand shot out to slap Delaney hard across the face. "I want you to leave...*now!*"

Delaney worked his jaw, his mouth thinning into a stubborn line. "I'm not going anywhere—"

"Then I will." Marina swiveled away from him to snatch the cordless phone from its cradle. That was when she noticed Reese's card wasn't next to the phone where she'd left it. She could've sworn she'd seen it there yesterday. Had that been before, or after, the blow to her head? Frowning, she scanned the counter again.

"Are you looking for this?"

She whirled around to find Reese's card perched between Delaney's index and middle fingers. Leveling him with a withering glare, she plucked the card from his hand, her fingers trembling as she punched the numbers into the phone. Four rings later, Reese still hadn't answered. *Please, please, please...pick up!* Marina frantically repeated the plea in her mind.

"He's not going to answer, Marina."

She took in the obstinate set of his jaw and realized the truth of it. "Oh, right...He's *your* employee." Her shoulders slumped forward in defeat as she carelessly jammed the phone back into its cradle. "How convenient."

"I had to do something, damn it!" Delaney's legendary composure snapped, his hands slashing through the air. "You haven't exactly been reasonable about any of this!"

"Me?" Marina snorted. "I'm not the one who got us into this mess, remember?" She shuffled over to the front door, one hand resting on her hip, the other reaching out to grasp the handle. "I agree with you, though. There's nothing reasonable about this situation." She yanked the door open. "That's why you need to leave."

"I'm afraid I'm not in a position to do that right now," Delaney remarked in a more modulated tone.

Marina felt a tremor of alarm skitter through her. "What's that supposed to mean?"

"I was dropped off here the same as you," he began, as if he were launching into a boardroom presentation at Argyle Media Solutions. "I gave Reese strict instructions not to answer calls from either one of us until Monday morning. That should give us sufficient time to discuss our, uh..." He waved a finger between the two of them. "I mean, to see how this is going to go."

Marina was too stunned to offer any objections.

"I'm afraid you're stuck with me for the next few days." Delaney shrugged casually. "Until things are settled between us."

Fury threatened to choke her, but somehow Marina managed to force words from her stiff lips. "Consider it settled then!"

Slamming the door behind her, Marina fled the cabin.

11

*M*arina had no idea where she was going.

But her physical need to be away from Foster Delaney propelled her down the dirt and gravel drive. Her hands clenched reflexively at her sides; her lungs burned from exertion and anger; her head pounded with each step she took. She should be relaxing in the cabin, not dodging muddy puddles on a rain-slicked road.

But she couldn't stay there. Not now. She didn't know what made her angrier, Delaney's appalling reason for following her to Ogunquit, or the way her body had reacted to his touch. She hated to admit how far she would've allowed Delaney's seduction to go had his revelation, and her subsequent anger, not intervened. The mere brush of his fingers along the nape of her neck had awakened something deep within her. Had it gone on one moment longer, she would surely have been lost. Fortunately, she'd managed to escape before her tenuous moral compass had totally shattered.

The worst of it was, she'd almost surrendered herself to a man who didn't respect or cherish her, who was interested in only a physical relationship with one of his employees. How could she have been so wrong about Foster Delaney? Had her experience with Grayson taught her nothing?

The pedestal she'd placed Delaney on had crumbled. As disappointing as that was, it might be the only way she could convince herself he was no good for her, that she should forget about him and move on.

Marina forced all thoughts of Delaney from her mind. She didn't have the energy to dwell on the matter with her ribs pinching her side and her head throbbing with every step she took. She'd changed back into her novelty slippers after returning from the drive to the clearing, and now the absurd blue doggies hugging her otherwise bare feet impeded her progress as she stumbled along the sodden, rut-pocked road.

"Ouch!" she yelped, as a sharp rock dug into the sole of one of her house slippers. Glancing up at the blanket of heavy gray clouds overhead, she berated herself for leaving the cabin so abruptly without her cell phone, a pair of proper shoes, and a sturdy garment thicker than her delicate silk blouse. Thoughts of a sudden downpour made her feet move a little faster.

The distant rumble of an engine somewhere up ahead brought her to a stop. Squinting, she made out the silhouette of a small vehicle bouncing along the road. She tried to raise her arm to flag down the driver, only to jerk it back with a hiss of pain. Wrapping one arm around her ribs, she bent the other arm out at the elbow and folded her hand into the universal hitchhiking sign. But the little car sailed past her, splashing an arc of frigid muddy water down the front of her shirt and slacks.

"Seriously?" Marina choked back a bitter laugh as she plucked the sodden blouse away from her chilled skin. Folding her arms around her shivering body, she forced herself into motion again, wondering how much longer she'd have to walk. Why the devil hadn't she thought to take the golf cart? At the very least, she should've followed the forest trail at the back of Delaney's rental cabin that would supposedly take her to Lucas's place. She could use a friendly face about now. Not to mention a bonfire the size of Maine.

As it was, she was shivering with cold, and her teeth were chattering uncontrollably as she hobbled along the seemingly endless stretch of rain-pitted dirt road in mud-caked doggy slippers and sopping wet clothes.

She was so distracted by her thoughts, that she nearly missed the entrance to a narrow road, winding off to her left through thick clusters of pines. Worrying her bottom lip with her teeth, Marina warily glanced up and down the main road, considering her options. But when her gaze flitted back to the little side road, she spotted a thin column of smoke rising above the trees somewhere up ahead.

Marina had no idea who, or what, she might find at the end of that road, but her sore, chilled body had a mind of its own. And her feet were already carrying her toward the promise of warmth.

— ~

Marina stared at the weathered cabin nestled in the small wooded clearing. Compared to the luxury cabin she was staying in, the little cedar-sided house before her resembled an oversized Tuff Shed. A beat-up old pickup truck, the bumpers freckled with patches of rust, was parked to one side of the cabin.

It was probably the dwelling of some old hermit, she reasoned, her eyes darting between the humble shelter and the narrow road behind her. She was just about to step forward, out of the protective shadows of the trees, when the cabin door was flung open and a huge man stepped out into the hazy light of the cloudy afternoon.

She shrank back into the shadows, startled by the sheer size of him. The man definitely wasn't old. Nor did he resemble any hermit she'd ever seen. From her vantage point, she could tell he was handsome. OK, H-O-T was more like it. He held a coffee cup in one large hand, and the other hand stifled a yawn from a mouth framed by a chiseled, clean-shaven jaw. Craning her neck, she eyed the jeans that hugged his long toned legs and taut buttocks as if they were the skin he'd been born in. The blue and brown flannel shirt he wore hung open at the neck, revealing an enticing view of a muscled chest dusted with honey-colored hair.

Marina pursed her lips, head cocked. Something about the tawny demigod before her recalled to mind her meeting with Lucas the other night. Tony had referred to the man as the "yummy lumberjack," and Marina certainly thought it a fitting appellation for the masculine specimen her eyes now feasted upon. She could've ogled the man all afternoon had not a wolfish-looking beast suddenly appeared in the doorway of the cabin.

Wriggling around the man's large form, the excited canine shot straight for Marina as if it had spotted a forest critter in need of a good chasing. Stumbling backward, she stifled a yelp when the dog trotted up to her side and circled her feet, sniffing at her slippers, his tail thumping against her legs. She closed her eyes, gritting her teeth against the pain she might feel any moment when the beast decided to attack.

"What'd you find there, boy?"

She heard the sound of crunching gravel as the man approached. Glancing down at her sodden clothes and doggy slipper-clad feet, she muttered a curse. Why was it that she seemed destined to encounter handsome men under less than ideal wardrobe circumstances? Marina didn't know what was worse, having a stranger come upon her in a bare-ly-there swimsuit or feeling exposed by a drenched white blouse that clung to her skin and clearly outlined the bra underneath. At least it had been dark the night she'd met Lucas in her near-nothings.

"Hawk!" the man called out.

A soft gasp escaped her as realization dawned. Somehow, she'd unwittingly ended up at Lucas Reynolds's cabin. Any relief at happening upon someone familiar was quickly extinguished by embarrassment over the pitiful state of her appearance. She seriously considered taking cover behind a tree, but Hawk would no doubt give away her location. Wrapping her arms over her chest, she waited for the inevitable.

Lucas stopped dead in his tracks, chocolate-colored eyes going wide as his puzzled gaze traveled over her, lingering on her feet.

Marina felt her cheeks flush with heat. Humiliatingly conscious of his scrutiny, she struggled for words to distract him. "I'm so relieved to stumble upon someone I know..." Her gaze nervously followed Hawk, but the dog simply trotted away and busied himself with exploring the forest floor, muzzle to the ground. "I feel like I've been wandering around out here forever."

He scratched his head, eyebrows pinching into a frown. "I, uh—"

"We met the other night," she quickly interjected. "Your dog jumped into my hot tub."

"Marina?" Recognition flared behind Lucas's soft mocha eyes, his mouth curving into a wide grin. "I was hopin' you'd drop by."

"Well, here I am." Her voice trembled through chattering teeth. Rubbing her hands over her arms, she startled when Hawk loped back to her side, whimpering as if sensing her distress.

"Hawk's right." Lucas cocked his head toward the Tuff Shed. "We'd best get you inside. "What happened to you, anyway?"

"I'm afraid it's a rather long story." She smiled ruefully as they headed for shelter.

"Judgin' from how wet your clothes are," he drawled, his gaze sweeping over her, "you'll have plenty of time to tell me about it while you dry off."

❧

"This oughta warm you up." Lucas handed Marina a mug of hot chocolate.

"Thanks." She gratefully accepted the cup he offered, wrapping her hands around the chipped ceramic mug to absorb its heat. She snuggled deeper into the comfortable leather recliner that cradled her weary body, gazing into the cheery warmth of orange flames flickering in the stone fireplace only a few yards away. She'd shed her wet clothes and now wore one of Lucas's flannel shirts, with a patchwork quilt tucked around her lower body.

The cabin's interior was roomier than she would have guessed from the outside, with exposed wooden beams in the vaulted ceiling, reminiscent of an old English cottage. A smile touched her lips as her gaze roamed over the built-in bookcases flanking the fireplace, with paperbacks jammed every which way on the shelves.

But Marina's smile disappeared when she warily eyed the dog lounging at Lucas's feet near the hearth. When had the sneaky beast wandered into the room? She glanced up to find her host's sharp brown gaze appraising her.

"I can't help but notice you don't seem too fond of dogs," he observed. "Bad experience?"

"Dog attack." She shrugged it off, unwilling to admit to a virile man like Lucas that a tiny, yipping Pomeranian was the source of her absurd paranoia.

"Ah." He nodded in understanding. "Would it make you feel more comfortable if I put Hawk in the back room?"

He half rose from his chair, but Marina thrust up her hand. "That won't be necessary." She winced at how the gesture tweaked her sore ribs. "I need to learn to deal with it if I'm ever going to get over it."

Lucas's eyes narrowed suspiciously. "Looks to me like you're dealin' with a lot more than a fear of dogs." Setting his mug on the desk behind him, he leaned forward, resting his forearms on his knees. "Care to tell me what happened to you?"

— ~

For the second time since she'd arrived in Ogunquit, three days ago, Marina had just unburdened her ordeal with her employer upon yet another stranger.

"That's quite a story." Lucas whistled, leaning back in his chair.

"It's something, all right." She snorted. "A big. Fat. Mess."

"Normally I'm a fan of lettin' messes work themselves out." He rubbed at his chin. "In matters of love and relationships, though, I think it's best to be proactive."

Marina recoiled. "Are you saying I should've just jumped into bed with my boss?"

"What I'm sayin' is"—he tilted forward in his chair, lowering his voice meaningfully—"if I was your employer, I'd change company policy, say to hell with my hifalutin job, or do whatever else it took to make you mine."

His answer tugged at her heart. "That's very romantic of you."

The deep rumbling she heard building in Lucas's chest erupted in laughter, rousing Hawk from his slumber.

"What's so funny?"

He reached up, withdrew a paperback from the bookshelf, and lightly tossed it into her lap. "See for yourself." He gestured at the novel with a flick of his chin.

"*Autumn in Your Arms*," Marina murmured the book's title, admiring the cover. A young couple, bundled up in cozy-looking sweaters, jeans, and boots, lay facing one another in the bed of a hay wagon. The man's head was propped in his palm, the fingers of his other hand stretched out to wrap around a glistening chestnut curl of the woman's hair.

As Marina gazed at the book, the image changed, and she imagined *herself* lying next to Foster Delaney in the bed of hay, imagined *his* fingers winding through *her* hair. When she felt the little pang of longing in her heart, she quickly blinked away the fantasy, disconcerted at the direction her thoughts had taken. Shifting her attention to the author's name embossed across the bottom of the book, she traced her finger over the raised letters, her brows pulling together in confusion. "Fiona Highcourt?" she read aloud, glancing up at him questioningly.

"My pseudonym," he acknowledged with a sly grin. "Fiona's my sister's name. A guy's gotta have a little anonymity when he's writin' romances, you know?"

She choked down a mouthful of hot cocoa before it could spew from her lips. "Y...you're a romance writer?"

"Well, after a lifetime of observin' five sisters fall in love, romance writin' just seemed to come naturally." He reached down to scratch Hawk behind the ears. "You wouldn't know it by the looks of me. Isn't that right, boy?"

"It *is* rather hard to imagine a beefcake like you writing sappy love stories," Marina quipped.

"Beefcake, huh?" Lucas regarded her with amusement.

"Would you prefer yummy lumberjack?"

"Who calls me that?" he choked out, his handsome face pinched into a comic expression.

"Tony Carmichael."

"What a character." He chuckled, shaking his head. "When did you meet Tony?"

"I ran into him and Jake yesterday out on Marginal Way," she explained. "We had lunch in Perkins Cove."

"At the restaurant where Jake works?"

"I had the fried haddock," Marina said proudly. "And I don't even like fish."

"There isn't a bad dish on their menu," Lucas asserted. "Though I'm a steak man myself." He shifted forward in his chair again, a glint of curiosity flashing in his eyes. "So did Tony manage to ferret out your whole life story, includin' this business with your employer, before you parted company?"

"He has an unnatural talent for that sort of thing, doesn't he?" Marina responded drolly. "Luckily I managed to avoid his attempts at matchmaking, though."

"Oh?" One brow lifted in interest. "How's that?"

"I told him I'd already met *you*."

A self-satisfied smile tipped the corners of his mouth, and his chest puffed up slightly. "And what did Tony say?" He stood, motioning for Hawk to stay, and crossed over to her, holding out a hand for her empty mug.

"That we should 'hook up.'" Marina made an air quote with one hand, relinquishing the cup in her other hand. As she did so, her fingers brushed Lucas's, sending an enticing flutter of energy along her nerves. It was a milder sensation than the dizzying current of heat that had surged through her veins at Delaney's touch, but it was not an unpleasant one.

"Guess I shouldn't be surprised by anythin' that comes out of that man's mouth." Lucas's throaty laughter yanked her from her thoughts as he turned to carry both their mugs over to the kitchenette.

Marina cast a wary glance at Hawk to assure herself that he didn't intend to pounce on her when his master's back was turned. But the dog appeared more interested in a tendon chew toy at the moment, so she let her gaze roam back to Lucas, admiring the way his triceps muscles bunched as he washed out the mugs and set them in a plastic rack to drain.

"Well, you wouldn't hear me complainin' if we hooked up." He flicked the water from his hands, wiped them on his pant legs, and strode back over to the office chair. "But that's the difference between me and your bonehead boss." He smirked. "I know a good thing when I see it."

Marina offered him an appreciative smile, grateful for his humorous attempts at lightening the mood. But he must have sensed her wistfulness because his expression instantly shifted from one of amusement, to concern. "What're you goin' to do?"

"I'm not sure." She heaved a sigh. "But I can't stay at that cabin while *he's* there."

Lucas scratched his head. "Got another place in mind?"

She pursed her lips. "Well, when I stumbled upon your cabin, the plan was to use your phone to call Tony and have him come pick me up. But...I don't have his number with me."

"It wouldn't do you any good if you did." Lucas sounded strangely pleased. "I don't have a phone."

12

"You don't have a phone?" Marina blinked in disbelief. "Why not?"

"It's a distraction I don't need when I'm up here writin'." Lucas shrugged. "When I have my cell phone with me, everyone considers it a personal invitation to inundate me with calls and texts."

"But what if you had an emergency?" she protested.

"You mean like a concussed, mud-soaked woman wandering aimlessly along a deserted back road in search of a phone?"

"Very funny," Marina grumbled, finding it hard not to return his disarming smile. Her gaze shifted to his computer screen, sparking an idea. "Hey." Her smile brightened. "I could try and reach Tony through Skype!" But her excitement quickly faded.

"Shoot, I keep forgetting I don't have his business card with me." She frowned, checking her pockets as if she expected it to magically materialize there. "Honestly, I don't know why I had to go and leave my cell phone behind. If my stupid brain had been working, I wouldn't have run off like a complete idiot. Now what am I supposed to do?"

"Well, I'd be willing to—"

She heard Lucas's voice but barely registered his presence. She unconsciously rubbed at her temples as she continued to mutter under her breath. "I guess I could try to e-mail Erik. I'm sure he'd be willing to pick me up and drive me back to Portland."

As soon as the words slipped from her mouth, fleeting images of home skittered through her mind. Her cozy condo. The window seat where she liked to read. Evenings spent in the company of her dear friends, Erik and Jill. Even the aloof cat she shared her living space with. Suddenly Marina felt very homesick. As if that wasn't bad enough, her head chose that very moment to start throbbing again. Sagging against the back of the loveseat, she closed her eyes.

"You OK?" Lucas's deep voice rumbled near her face, his breath fanning her cheek.

Marina's eyes fluttered open to find him studying her uncertainly, eyebrows creased with worry. "I think I could use some Tylenol," she mumbled, lightly brushing the knot on her head with her fingers.

"Let me see what I've got." He hurried down the hall.

Marina heard the clink of a glass and the flow of water, and then Lucas was back, kneeling beside her. "Don't go feelin' like you have to rush off." He handed her the water. "You're more than welcome to stay here for as long as you need to."

She swallowed down the pills and handed the glass back to Lucas. Setting it aside, he took her small hand in his large, rough one, his gaze warm and earnest. "There's a loft." He pointed a finger somewhere above and behind her. "I can sleep up there, and you can take the bed."

Regardless of how innocent the circumstances were, Marina experienced a moment of doubt as she stared down at their joined hands. A glance at the high windows on the back wall revealed a darkened sky. What else was she to do? Without a cell phone, she had no way of contacting her friends to come retrieve her, and it might be a while before they arrived anyway. Besides, her body was tired from its ordeal, and Lucas's cabin was so warm and cozy.

"Has anyone ever told you how adorable it is when you gnaw on your bottom lip like that?"

"Nervous habit." Marina shrugged, pressing her lips together to re-sist the temptation of biting them again.

"I can think of a better way to keep them occupied."

The mischief glittering in Lucas's dark eyes turned hot, and Marina felt her face flush with warmth.

"Sorry." He released her hand and propped his own on the arm of the chair. "I didn't mean to embarrass you." Resting his chin in the palm of his hand, he sighed. "Listen, you don't have to decide anythin' right now. Just rest for a while, OK? Then, if you're still not comfortable with the idea of a slumber party with a yummy lumberjack, I'll drive you wherever you wanna go, even back to Portland."

His offer touched her, but it was overly generous. He'd been so kind to her already. She gave her sore head a gentle shake. "I couldn't ask you to do that."

"Well, you didn't," he pointed out. "I volunteered."

Marina bit down on her lip to keep it from trembling, her emotions a chaotic mix of exhaustion from her injury, frustration over her or-deal with Delaney, and gratitude for Lucas's kindness. Impulsively, she leaned forward to press a kiss to his cheek.

But Lucas captured her face in his hands and claimed her mouth instead.

His kiss was warm, sweet and minty, like the hot chocolate they'd just drank. Delicate as the caress was, it did not lack for passion, send-ing a delicious little tingle along her skin. It was thrilling to think Lucas found her desirable. He was witty, honest, kind, and gorgeous. Unlike her enigmatic, very off-limits employer, Lucas was just the sort of man she needed in her life right now, the type of man she *should* be in love with.

Only...she wasn't.

The realization shot through her as if her veins had been injected with ice water. She broke the kiss and straightened away from Lucas.

For the space of a second, he seemed unaware that the kiss had end-ed. Then his eyes snapped open and he cursed, raising himself onto the ottoman in front of her. "I'm sorry," he shoved a hand through his thick mane of tawny hair. "I shouldn't have done that. You're vulnerable. Not to mention, in love with another man."

He was right. She *was* vulnerable. Normally, she wasn't the type of woman who went around kissing men she'd only just met, no matter how hot they were. But as of late, nothing about her life—or her time in Ogunquit—had been normal. And anyway, Lucas no longer felt like a stranger. Not after experiencing his gentle care as he'd seen to her warmth and comfort, and his genuine concern as he'd patiently listened to her pour out her heart about her employer. No, Lucas felt like more than someone she'd met only twice, and she'd be lying if she said his kiss had been completely unwelcome. Who *wouldn't* want to kiss a guy like him?

The problem was, when Lucas kissed her, she'd been thinking about what it would feel like to kiss Foster Delaney. So clearly, now wasn't the right time to be kissing lumberjacks. No matter how kind or yummy they were. "Don't worry about it." Marina waved off his apology and settled back against the recliner. "Just don't let it happen again," she teased.

"Wow, OK." Lucas snorted. "That bad, huh?"

"It didn't totally suck."

"Gee, thanks." He grimaced. "Being a romance writer, I always assumed I had a particular gift for kissing. Until today, that is."

"Oh, you're *very* gifted." Marina blushed. "And I probably would've been more responsive if it weren't for—" The last words stuck in her throat. *A certain boss of mine.*

"Whoever this idiot is"—Lucas's expression softened—"I hope he wakes up and realizes what he's got before it's too late."

"Thanks for saying so." She forced a smile to her lips. "But I don't see that happening." Foster Delaney had made it very clear what he wanted from her outside of their professional relationship. Now she understood the implications of the impromptu vacation and the luxury accommodations. But she still struggled to reconcile the reckless man who wanted to engage in a casual, albeit unseemly, fling with his employee with the respectable, thoughtful, and generous man she'd come to admire and adore.

Regardless of what Marina thought of Delaney's less than noble intentions, she still found herself wondering if he'd worried about her since she'd fled the cabin. Would he come looking for her? She knew it was foolish to ponder such things. At the end of the day, Foster Delaney was still her employer. Not to mention insensitive, and a womanizer—a trait he apparently had in common with her ex. So why was she still wasting energy thinking about him? Forcing all thoughts of Delaney from her head, Marina refocused her attention on Lucas.

"Well, if he doesn't," he was saying, playfully jostling her knee with his own, "I'll be happy to knock the livin' daylights out of him before I step in to woo you myself."

"*Woo* me?" Marina's brows wrinkled in amusement, her chest twitching with the need to laugh. "I didn't think modern men actually used that term anymore."

"In my defense"—Lucas flashed her a goofy grin—"I'm a sappy romance writer, remember?"

"Valid point." Her gaze suddenly darted around the room, a shiver of irrational panic skittering through her. "Um, where's Hawk?"

"Probably back in the bedroom." Lucas shrugged. "Guess he got bored of watchin' us make out."

"We weren't making out!" Marina grimaced. "On the other hand, if that's what it takes to scare off ankle-biting canines, I might have to try kissing a stranger whenever I find myself in the presence of dogs."

"I'd like to officially volunteer my services as your kissing partner." He waggled his brows.

Marina couldn't help the giggle that bubbled out of her. "I'll keep that in mind." His answering laughter, deep and throaty, settled over her like a balm. Once again, she found herself wondering why she couldn't have met him *before* Foster Delaney had swooped in to stake his claim on her heart—a portion of which she feared would always belong to him, wrong though it was. Why was she so blasted willing to swing open the door of her heart to men like Grayson and Delaney while perfectly nice men like Lucas were left standing out on the porch?

When she'd left Portland on Thursday, she'd done so with a renewed determination to make a clean break from her emotional ties to Delaney. Perhaps it was time to "loosen up" as Tasha and Jill had always told her. While she typically didn't engage in one-night stands or meaningless flings, Marina couldn't deny that a no-strings-attached vacation romance with Lucas might be just what she needed to help her move on. He was funny, clever and gorgeous. And he made her feel appreciated and sexy. Still, she couldn't help feeling a little stab of guilt for even thinking about it.

Surfacing from her ruminations, Marina was relieved to find that Lucas's flirty mood had passed. She wasn't entirely sure she liked the serious look on his face, though. He looked like a man who had plans of his own.

"You know..." Lucas leveled an assessing gaze at her. "I'm thinkin' I might be able to help you work through this dog issue. If you're interested, that is."

Apprehension knotted in Marina's stomach. "Oh. I, uh—"

"It was only a suggestion." He held up a hand to halt her forthcoming objection. "No pressure."

She chewed at her bottom lip, recalling how Erik had tried to help cure her dog phobia as well. In the end, his efforts had been unsuccessful. It was entirely possible that Lucas would fail, too. On the other hand, if she could conquer this obstacle, perhaps it would give her the courage she needed to tackle larger ones, like severing her emotional apron strings with Delaney. Heaven knew she could use all the help she could get where her employer was concerned.

Even now, knowing Delaney's intentions for following her to Ogunquit, she still felt a twinge of longing for him. It was ridiculous, she knew, but she couldn't seem to help it. *Enough!* she silently scolded herself. It was time for an intervention, and working through her canine neurosis would require the whole of her concentration, energy, and courage. There would be no room left for thoughts of Foster Delaney.

Before she could change her mind, Marina forced the words out of her mouth. "Let's do this."

Atta girl! Marina thought she heard Tasha's voice whisper in her head. Like the big scaredy-cat she was, though, her resolve almost crumbled in the next instant when she heard Lucas call, "Hawk, come!"

She'd forgotten how at ease she'd become with the dog out of sight, but now her anxiety had returned in full force. It didn't matter that Lucas was in the room or that she knew he wouldn't let Hawk hurt her. The instant Hawk loped into view, her hands clenched tightly at the arms of the recliner, and her heart started thudding in her chest. She could have sworn his penetrating blue eyes—which were locked on her— gleamed with the wicked anticipation of a predator about to mess with its prey.

In that moment of paralyzing fear, all thoughts of Foster Delaney evaporated.

13

"*I* can't believe it!" Marina beamed, rubbing Hawk behind the ears where his head lolled against her thigh. "This is the closest I've been to a dog since my attack in April."

"You're a good student." Lucas smiled approvingly. "It also helps that this particular canine is an old softie when it comes to women, especially ones with shapely ankles." He winked at her.

She blushed at his compliment and dropped her gaze to the dog at her side. If Erik could see her now! Had someone told her yesterday that, in the next twenty-four hours she'd be snuggling with a dog, let alone merely petting one, Marina would have laughed in that person's face. Even with Hawk cuddled up next to her, she was still having a hard time believing it herself.

Lucas had achieved this small miracle with a great deal of prudence and patience. He'd started off having Hawk sit as near to her as she'd allow, giving her time to become comfortable with the canine's proximity. Inch by inch, he'd moved the animal closer, until he was near enough to touch. Then, with the dog's head turned away from her, Lucas had instructed Marina to pet Hawk's body without the intimidation of seeing his mouth and worrying what he might do. When she'd grown accustomed to that, Lucas had held Hawk's collar while she'd experimented with petting behind his ears and the top of his head. Finally, he'd encouraged her to let the dog sniff at her hand and lick it with his tongue. And now, here they sat, as if Hawk had always been her pet instead of Lucas's.

The entire process had taken several hours, and in that time, Marina had decided what she needed to do. She planned to take Lucas up on his offer to stay the night. But In the morning, she'd ask him drive her to the rental cabin so she could collect her things. From there, she'd call Erik, and then have Lucas take her into town, where she'd check into a hotel and wait for Erik to come pick her up. As she mulled the plan over in her head, Marina became aware of Lucas's gaze upon her.

"Mind if I ask you a question about this boss of yours?" he asked when she looked up.

Delaney was the last person Maria wanted to talk about at the moment. The past few hours had been pleasantly Delaney-free and she had no wish to sour the mood by revisiting the subject of her employer. At the same time, she was curious to know what kind of insights Lucas could offer on the matter. After all, he'd observed five sisters pass through the elation and heartache of love. And anyway, he'd helped her work through her fear of dogs. The least she could do was answer his questions.

"OK." She nodded.

"What is it about this guy that has you so enthralled?"

Her lips curved into a humorless smile at his choice of words. *Everything* about the man captivated her. Or, at least, it used to. But so much had happened over the past few days to make Marina doubt what she knew about Delaney. So why did she still find him so annoyingly appealing?

"Marina?"

"Sorry." She shook her head, rubbing at her temple. "It's a lot of things, really." She told him of her employer's generosity throughout her sister's illness and passing, of the way she felt when she danced with him at the summer kickoff party. She spoke of the personal conversation they'd engaged in at the pub and the jade dolphin Delaney had given her. And she told him of the personal connection that had passed between them in the druid clearing earlier in the day.

But one experience in particular flooded her with bittersweet memories, and she found the words tumbling out of her mouth. "About a month or so after my sister passed away, I was having a really horrible day at work. I couldn't focus, couldn't stop crying. I was completely nonfunctional."

Lucas leaned forward, resting his forearms on his knees.

Marina told him how Delaney had followed her to the park that day. "He didn't try to placate me with clichés or convince me everything would be OK, you know? He simply sat with me, in the freezing cold—for who knows how long—until I felt composed enough to return to the office. I don't think there are a lot of men out there who would be willing to do that."

"And you've been fallin' in love with him ever since?" Lucas asked softly.

Marina's startled gaze flew to Lucas's face, her hand stilling on Hawk's head. "I-I don't know." The dog whimpered, and she commenced rubbing his ears again. "All I know for sure is that's when my feelings for him started changing in a fundamental way."

"Do you think he's aware of how you really feel about him?"

She had wondered that same thing on more than one occasion. After today, she had no doubt Delaney knew just how attracted she was to him. The sexual tension that had flared between them had been unmistakable. But as to whether he recognized her deep affection for him, she couldn't say. As far as she knew, he would just use it to his advantage to get her into his bed.

Her gaze followed her hands as they traced lazy patterns in Hawk's thick coat. It was a methodic gesture she found strangely comforting. "I don't think it matters at this point," she told Lucas. "But why do you ask?"

"Because the more I've had time to think about it"—he stroked his chin, regarding her carefully—"the more I suspect your feelings are precisely the reason he's here."

Marina looked at him askance. "What do you mean?"

"I'm thinkin' it's very likely your employer's in love with you, too."
He tapped Marina's quilt-covered knee meaningfully with his index
finger. "He's probably here to tell you that very thing so you can, you
know, take the relationship to the next level."

"There. Is. No. Relationship." Marina enunciated each word. "I
told you what he did, what he said."

"Believe me"—he grimaced—"I know how this must be soundin' to
you."

Yeah, she massaged her temple. *It sounds an awful lot like something Erik
would say.* Her friend, too, had suggested that Delaney cared for her,
going so far as to insist that they belonged together. Something else
Erik had said floated back to her. *A guy can tell when another guy has it bad
for a woman.*

But there was no way Lucas could know such a thing. He'd never
even met Delaney. Of course, that might just be the romance author
in him speaking. As for her part, she was certain Lucas, like Erik, was
wrong about Delaney. He did not love her, and she was done talking
about it, so sick and tired of even thinking about it. Marina felt suddenly weary and wished for nothing more than the peaceful numbness
of sleep.

"Um, if you don't mind," she yawned out, "I think I'll take you up on
your offer to stay the night."

"Of course." Lucas was immediately on his feet. "Come on, Hawk.
Let Marina up."

Hawk whined as she shifted forward in the chair, shoving aside the
quilt. "Sorry, boy." She stroked his head affectionately. "It's been a long
day, and I'm ready for bed."

"I'm surprised you made it this long," Lucas remarked, extending a
hand to help her up. No sooner had he managed to get Marina to her
feet, than a fierce pounding rattled the cabin door.

Marina let out a yip of surprise, tightening her grip on Lucas's arm.
Hawk assumed a protective stance next to Marina, a low, menacing growl
rumbling in his throat.

"Easy, you two." Lucas chuckled, hitching his thumb toward the door. "Whaddya wanna bet that's a certain frantic employer who's been out searchin' for you?"

Hope made Marina's heart beat erratically. Surely Delaney wouldn't have bothered to come looking for her if she meant nothing more to him than a casual hookup, right? Was it possible that he actually cared for her as Lucas had suggested? Either way, she wasn't ready to deal with Foster Delaney tonight.

The cabin door trembled under another furious pummeling. Marina winced at the sound, calming an agitated Hawk with a few strokes of her hand as she glanced between Lucas and the door.

"Any chance I can convince you *not* to open that door?" she muttered pleadingly.

Her reaction seemed to amuse him. "And miss out on all the fun I could have, if it happens to be who I think it is?" Lucas shook his head, flashing her a wicked grin. "Not a chance."

Before Marina could react, Lucas shoved her behind him so she was mostly concealed by the door and his broad back. Reaching for the door knob, he gave her a quick wink over his shoulder. "Watch and enjoy."

⌐ ⌐

"If you're done beatin' the hell out of my door now..." Lucas greeted the visitor, casually leaning against the doorjamb, one arm resting above his head. "What can I help you with?"

"The name's Foster Delaney." The familiar self-possessed voice floated through the narrowly opened door, mingling with the sound of a car's running engine. "I'm looking for a woman."

Lucas leaned forward slightly, glancing out the door. "You're the one runnin' around in fancy clothes and a million-dollar limo. I'm surprised you can't find a woman on your own."

Limo? Marina mouthed the word, scrunching up her face. Delaney had told her he'd instructed the chauffeur to refuse his calls until Monday. Apparently, he'd lied about that, too. Of course, he was a powerful and resourceful man. No doubt he was practiced at getting exactly *what* he wanted, *when* he wanted it. Including extracurricular favors from his employees.

She shook her head, still struggling to wrap her head around Erik's and Lucas's assumption that Delaney wanted more than that from her. He sure hadn't been acting like it lately. Tony had told her that love makes us all a little crazy. Well, crazy certainly fit Delaney's odd behavior over the past week, but she doubted it had anything to do with love.

"She's about five seven and slender." Delaney's voice pierced through her introspection. "Long, glossy black hair, crystal blue eyes, alabaster skin..."

Marina's eyes widened at his description of her features, but it was his raspy voice that moved over her like a caress, making her tremble inside. Suddenly, she felt an overpowering urge to see him. Craning her neck to peek through the small space between Lucas's head and shoulder, she caught a glimpse of Delaney under the porch light. He wore the same ivory sweater from earlier, but he'd added a black leather jacket that, together with his whisker-shadowed jaw and disheveled hair, gave him a sexy, bad-boy appearance that made her heart stop.

She shifted her position to get a better view of him, and was shocked to see that, under the porch light's glow, his face was ashen, his features tense, and his lips were drawn into a tight line. He looked so tired, haggard even. Had he been out searching for her all day? Guilt pricked at her and she opened her mouth to say something.

But Lucas beat her to it.

"Sounds like a real beauty," he trumpeted appreciatively. Straightening his intimidating form away from the doorjamb, he folded his arms over his puffed-out chest. "Whaddya want with her?"

"That's my business," Delaney answered coolly.

"What's her name?"

"Marina. Thatcher. She's my employee. Uh, I mean... she's, well, a friend of mine."

"Sounds to me," Lucas drawled, "like you're not sure *who* you're lookin' for."

Delaney ignored Lucas's glib comment. "I talked with a resident who claimed he saw a woman who fits Marina's description out on the main road earlier today. Have you seen her?"

Lucas inspected his fingernails as if bored with the conversation, but there was a hard edge to his voice. "If I had, it's not information I'd be sharin' with *you.*"

"You're a regular pain in the ass, you know that?" Delaney retorted.

Marina couldn't believe her ears. It was the snarkiest thing she had ever heard her employer say to anyone, even to Erik, who teased and provoked him incessantly.

Lucas seemed equally amused by Delaney's reaction. "Only when boneheads like you show up on my porch demandin' information they're not entitled to."

"I don't have time for this," Delaney muttered impatiently. "Have you seen her or not?"

"Let me think..." Lucas scratched his head.

Marina bit at her lip. It wasn't that she didn't appreciate how Lucas was looking out for her, or that her employer didn't deserve everything her host was dishing out, but for some reason she couldn't guess at— Delaney's haggard appearance, maybe?—she couldn't stand there any longer and listen to Lucas antagonize him.

Before she could change her mind, she reached up to tap Lucas's shoulder. "It's OK," she said in a clear, steady voice. "I'll talk to him."

"Whatever you say, darlin'." Lucas held the door open wider for Delaney to enter. Hawk snarled as he stepped into the cabin, staying close by Marina's side.

Delaney's brows arched questioningly. "I thought you were afraid of dogs."

"Lucas has been helping me work through it." She shrugged.

His eyes flicked between her and Lucas before settling, disapprovingly, somewhere below her waist. "From the looks of it, he's helping you with quite a bit more than that."

Following the direction of his fixed gaze, Marina sucked in a sharp breath. She'd completely forgotten that she wore nothing more than

Lucas's flannel shirt, the hem of which hit her midthigh. Heat flooded her face until she was certain her cheeks would catch fire.

"My clothes were wet," she mumbled.

"I let you in my house because that's what Marina wanted," Lucas warned Delaney. "But it doesn't mean I won't toss you right back out on your ass if you upset her."

"I apologize." Although he spoke to Marina, his steely green glare was leveled on Lucas. When his eyes shifted back to her face, his expression had softened. He reached out to place a hand on her shoulder but thought better of it when Hawk bared his teeth in a warning snarl. Delaney instinctively stepped back.

"How are you feeling?" he asked, his wary gaze flicking between her and the dog.

"Achy and tired," she admitted. "Lucas was helping me to bed when you arrived." The words were barely out of her mouth before Marina realized how bad they must sound to Delaney.

"*Bed?*" His voice was low and barely controlled. "*His* bed?" he growled, jutting a finger at Lucas.

"That's generally where one goes around here when one wants to *sleep.*" Lucas emphasized the latter word with a smirk. "It's a very comfortable mattress, my guests tell me."

A muscle quivered at Delaney's jaw. "Marina already has a place to sleep," he replied curtly. "And I assure you, it's more comfortable than anything you can offer her."

"Will you two just stop!" Marina tried to interrupt, but it was as if she weren't even in the room.

"If you're referrin' to that fancy pants cabin you rented," Lucas scoffed, "you oughta' know that luxury accommodations won't buy Marina's affections."

"How the hell would you know?" Delaney challenged him. "You've known her for all of what—a few hours?"

"Met her the night she arrived," Lucas shot back smugly. "Best damn night of my life." He cast Marina a meaningful glance and winked.

The look on Delaney's face was murderous. He took a step toward Lucas, his hands clenching at his sides, his eyes sparking green fire. But her host merely regarded her employer's displeasure with a self-satisfied smirk.

Marina rolled her eyes heavenward. The two men were so preoccupied with flinging insults at each other, it was as if she and Hawk didn't exist. Glancing down at the dog, she heaved out a sigh. "C'mon boy." She turned and headed for the bedroom. "Who knows how long this will go on?"

— ⁓

Moments later, dressed in her own clothes, Marina closed the bedroom door behind her so Hawk wouldn't follow her out. She could hear Lucas and Delaney still going at it and knew she couldn't stay at Luca's for the night. But she didn't feel comfortable staying at the cabin either.

With tensions running high, it would be in everyone's best interest—including her own—for her to stay at a hotel.If Reese was waiting outside, he could take her back to the cabin to retrieve her things and drive her into town.

Fatigue was tugging at every muscle in her body, and all she wanted to do was find neutral ground where she could take a hot bath and fall into bed. Tomorrow she'd head back to Portland. At the moment, though, she just wanted to get away from the drama. She'd had quite enough of that over the past few days.

Quietly, she walked past the bickering men and slipped out the door to the waiting limo.

14

"Miss Marina!" Reese exclaimed when she slipped into the back seat of the limo. "Thank heavens you're all right. Mr. Delaney's been awfully worried, and I was, too."

"Thank you, Reese." She winced at the little stab of guilt his statement had elicited, casting a quick glance back at Lucas's cabin. "It's been a rather tiresome day, and I'd really like to head back to the rental cabin now."

"Yes, I imagine you're plumb tuckered out." He tilted his head in question. "Will Mr. Delaney be joining us?"

"He's having, um, a *friendly* conversation with my rescuer. I'm afraid it could go on for a while."

"I see." The elderly chauffeur's eyes glinted with amusement. "I only caught a glimpse of him, but he looked to be a handsome sort of fellow. Intimidating, too. Probably rubbed Delaney the wrong way, I'll wager."

Marina half smiled and half grimaced to herself. *Oh yeah, Lucas was really good at that.* Nibbling at her lip, she voiced the question on her mind. "Would you be willing to drive me into town after I collect my things from the cabin? I'll be staying at a hotel tonight."

Reese's brows drew downward in a frown. "Is everything all right, Miss Marina?"

"It's just Marina," she admonished. "And no, not really."

The chauffeur's face visibly fell, but he gave a quick bob of his head. "All right then, I'll come back for Mr. Delaney while you pack your things."

"Thank you, Reese." She exhaled a sigh of relief as he pulled onto the main road, feeling some of the tension ease from her body as they put more distance between them and Lucas's cabin. Thoughts of a hot bath and a soft bed swirled through her head, tugging at her tired body.

The chauffeur's voice dragged her from her thoughts. "I don't suppose you've had much of a chance to discuss your, uh...that is, to talk with Mr. Delaney?"

"Actually, talking to him is kind of what landed me in this silly predicament." She tried to make light of it, but she was afraid her laugh came off more bitter than she'd intended.

"I don't mean to speak out of turn, Miss—I'm sorry— Marina. But..." He hesitated.

"Go on," she prompted warily.

"I know Mr. Delaney seems a bit out of sorts right now, but I'm sure there's a good reason for it."

Marina blew out a frustrated breath. Why did everyone seem to be taking Delaney's side? At one point, even Lucas had hinted that Delaney's intentions might be honorable after all. It seemed she was the only one who'd had the stars knocked out of her eyes where her employer was concerned. As if to prove her point, Reese chose that very moment to launch into a pro-Delaney speech.

"Mr. Delaney's a real gentleman," he declared, his black cap bobbing up and down on his head in a yes-siree nod. "Not too many like *him* these days."

Gentleman.

A week ago that's exactly how Marina would've described him, too. But too much had happened since then to convince her otherwise.

Reese, on the other hand, seemed to be suffering from a serious case of hero worship. "After I was fired from my hotel concierge position for an indiscretion I didn't commit"—he paused, his face crumpling as he recalled the bitter memory—"there wasn't a hotel anywhere else in the city that would hire me."

Marina knew instinctively what Reese would say next, and she didn't want to hear it. Another story extolling Delaney's virtues would only muddle her thinking and weaken her resolve.

"A friend of mine suggested I contact Mr. Delaney, knowing him to be a fair man. Sure enough, Mr. Delaney didn't judge me based on what had happened at that other hotel. He gave me a job, with full benefits, and when he found out about my wife's MS—" Reese stopped midsentence, his voice growing thick. "Well, let's just say he was very generous."

It was nothing she hadn't heard time and time again. She herself had experienced Delaney's kindness on a number of occasions. But why was Reese bothering to regale her with tales of her employer's benevolence now?

As if he'd read her mind, the chauffeur proceeded to answer her unspoken question. "Mr. Delaney has told me an awful lot about you." He caught her eye in the rearview mirror. "From what I can tell, you're not all that different from him. You're kind, compassionate, and willing to give people the benefit of the doubt."

Marina's jaw dropped open in astonishment. She couldn't imagine Delaney wanting to tell his chauffeur anything remotely pleasant about her, not after everything that had happened between them. Even more surprising, though, was Reese's glowing opinion of her character.

She hung her head, dismay knotting in her stomach. She was *not* the person he'd described.

After all, since her arrival in Ogunquit, she'd given virtual strangers more consideration and trust than she'd been willing to give Foster Delaney, the man who'd shown her such compassion and generosity during Tasha's illness and passing. Had she misjudged him?

After everything Delaney had done for her, the least she could do was give him a chance to explain himself, without jumping to conclusions or assuming the worst of him. She made a silent promise to give Delaney that opportunity first thing in the morning.

If he managed to make it out of Lucas's cabin in one piece tonight.

Marina had barely slipped into a clean bra and matching panties when her bedroom door flew open. She gasped, throwing her arms over her chest, simultaneously cursing the lack of two more arms to fling protectively around her nether region. "Don't you knock?"

"Not in my own—" He stopped midsentence, blinking rapidly, as if suddenly registering what he was seeing. Heat flickered briefly in his eyes before he turned away. "Sorry," he muttered. Marina hastily grabbed for her robe, her cheeks blazing hotter than the steamy bath she'd indulged in while waiting for Reese to return for her. Unfortunately, she hadn't bothered to finish dressing before she'd started tossing her things in the suitcase that lay open upon her bed.

Tying the flimsy, terry cloth garment securely around her middle with a fierce tug, she infused her voice with as much poise as she could muster, considering her employer had just seen her in her underwear. "OK, I'm decent." But she still felt self-conscious in the threadbare covering wrapped snuggly around her form.

"I apologize for barging in without knocking." Delaney turned to her, hands held out in a conciliatory gesture. "I just wanted to make sure you'd made it back all right before I turned in for the night." His eyes settled on the open suitcase, a frown flitting across his features. "What are you doing?"

Marina ignored his question. "Didn't Reese tell you he dropped me off when he came back for you?"

"I haven't seen him." He shook his head. "I walked here."

"Why would you do that?" She gaped at him. "Reese was on his way to pick you up. Anyway, now that you've obviously reinstated his services ahead of schedule, couldn't you have just called him on your cell phone to come get you?"

"It died." He grimaced, shifting his weight slightly to the right.

Marina's eyes narrowed at the way he favored his left leg. "What's wrong?"

"It's nothing," he said dismissively.

"Let me see." She dropped to her haunches, ignoring his protests. Lifting up his pant leg, she could see that his ankle was swollen. He wobbled on his feet as she gently removed his sock.

"Sit down, before you fall down." When he'd settled on the corner of her bed, she cradled his injured foot, wincing at the mass of ugly purplish bruises that marred his flesh. She couldn't believe he'd hobbled home and struggled up the stairs—on what must be a very painful sprain—to see after *her* welfare. It awakened the caretaking instincts she'd buried deep within her when Tasha had passed away, making her want to look after him just as he'd done for her when she'd become concussed. But before she could do anything about it, Reese's frantic shout rang out from downstairs.

"Mr. Delaney!"

"Up here!" He called out. Gingerly extracting his foot from Marina's hands, Delaney limped from her bedroom.

Marina followed him out to the landing where they met the red-faced chauffeur. "I'm terribly sorry I missed you, sir." Reese panted. "After dropping Miss Marina off, I headed back to Mr. Reynolds's place, but he said you'd already gone. I didn't see you along the road, and when I tried reaching you on your cell phone—"

Delaney held up a hand to silence the elderly gentleman, who appeared on the verge of hyperventilating. "It's not your fault, Reese."

The chauffeur visibly relaxed, his pale blue gaze shifting between Delaney and Marina. "I take it you won't be needing that ride into town now?" One white eyebrow tilted upward, his eyes alight with a curious twinkle.

Marina followed Reese's speculative gaze, groaning inwardly as she took in her appearance. Dressed in her robe, with her skin still slightly flushed from her employer coming upon her in her underwear, and still clutching Delaney's sock in her hand, she realized that the old man probably thought she and Delaney had been doing some "reconciling." She shook her head, wondering if the day could get any more humiliating.

"What?" Delaney's gaze shot to Marina's face. "You were leaving?"

Marina ignored his question and quickly turned to Reese. "Mr. Delaney has sprained his ankle. Please help him downstairs and get his leg elevated." Her voice rang with the authority of an experienced medical professional. "I'll be down as soon as I change. In the meantime, give him some ibuprofen and get an ice pack on that ankle."

Marina almost laughed at the expression of consternation on both their faces as she ordered them about. But it was a role she felt comfortable playing after long months of caring for Tasha. First, though, she needed to throw on some clothes. She wasn't about to nurse Delaney's ankle in her flimsy robe.

Blushing, she shoved Delaney's sock into Reese's hand and hastily retreated to her bedroom to change.

— ⌣

"You still haven't told me why you felt compelled to walk home." Marina adjusted the pillows behind the now reclining Delaney and checked his ice pack to make sure it didn't need changing.

His injured foot, resting upon a pillow, was propped up on the coffee table, near the dolphin figurine she'd left there the night before. Pursing her lips, Marina shifted his elevated foot a safe distance from the jade sculpture.

"Ouch!" Delaney growled. "What did you do that for?"

She pointed at the dolphin. "Just want to make sure you don't accidentally bump it or something."

"Oh, well...that's OK then." His lips twitched with a hint of a smile. "After all, from my vantage point, the view *was* pretty amazing. I don't think I've ever seen you wear jeans before. It suits you."

Marina glanced over her shoulder to find him appraising her behind with an appreciative glint in his eyes. She shook her head in bemusement. When she'd hastily pulled on a loose-fitting sweater and a plain old pair of Levis before coming downstairs, she'd never imagined Delaney would actually find them sexy—regardless of Jill's claim that she had a great butt for jeans—but she liked that fact that he did. A little too much.

Before that thought could go any further, she cleared her throat and asked, "So, are you going to tell me why you walked home, or not?" she asked

"I'll tell you on one condition," he said authoritatively.

"You're hardly in a position to be ordering me around." She regarded him with an amused smirk. "But if you ask again, nicely—"

"I was only going to point out that you're probably not in any condition to be fussing over me after the day you've had." Delaney gestured to the cushion next to him. "Please sit down. The ibuprofen's kicking in, and I'm quite comfortable, so you might as well be, too."

"All right," Marina agreed, lowering herself to the sofa. When she did so, she was surprised to find that their bodies were touching, from shoulders to knees. It did strange things to her senses and she wondered if he felt the same way. Casting him a sideways glance, she cleared her throat. "So..." she prompted. "You walked home because why?"

"Because, after your brute of a friend realized you were gone, he promptly ushered me out the door saying there was no longer any reason for me to stick around. When I pointed out that it was dark and my ride was gone, he told me to take the path through the forest. He just shoved a flashlight at my chest and slammed the door in my face. By that point, my cell phone was already dead, so I started walking. I hadn't been on the trail more than ten minutes or so when my foot slipped into a deep furrow and...well, you know the rest." He swept a hand toward his injured ankle.

"I'm so sorry," Marina said guiltily.

Delaney shook his head. "You're not to blame for any of this mess."

"But if I hadn't run off in the first place—" she protested.

"No." Delaney cut her off. "It's my fault. I've gone about this whole thing all wrong."

Marina turned her head to study him. As furious as she'd been with him earlier in the day, it surprised her that she didn't feel any gratification over his current distress. Instead, his vulnerability tugged at her heart. "Gone about what all wrong?" She laid her hand over his, where it rested on his thigh. "Is there something I can do to help?"

She felt him tense for the briefest moment, and then his hand was curling around her fingers. "Marina," he breathed out her name as he tilted his head and touched his forehead to hers. "You must know how I feel about you."

"There have been times when I thought I knew." Marina pulled back slightly, her gaze searching his features for answers. "But, I-I'm confused."

Delaney nodded his understanding. "Let me see if I can clear that up for you." He looked down at their joined hands and softy ran the pad of his thumb over her knuckles. "I've been smitten with you since the day you started working at Argyle. God knows I've tried not to be, for the obvious work-related reasons, and because you were with Grayson." He shook his head, his gaze shifting back to her face. "When I heard you weren't with him anymore, I began to hope—." He broke off midsentence and tried again. "The point is, I don't want there to be any more confusion between us. I love you, Marina. That's the reason I came here."

That was the reason he was here? Marina could hardly believe it. The man sure had a peculiar way of showing his devotion. Once again, Tony's words floated through her head...*Love makes us all a little crazy.* A slow smile began to tug at her lips. *Foster Delaney was in love with her!*

"Marina?"

The sound of his anxious voice brought her back to the present.

"Please tell me I'm not the only one feeling this way."

"No,"she whispered past the lump in her throat. "No, you're not."

Framing his face in her hands, she pressed her lips to his and let her kiss convey all the emotions she couldn't voice.

15

Their lips moved together and everything about it felt right. But Marina needed him closer. Threading her fingers through his hair, she deepened the kiss.

Growling low in his throat, Delaney's arm wrapped around her waist and crushed her against his chest. "I'm not hurting your ribs, am I?"

He was, but she wasn't about to tell him that now. "Stop talking," Marina rasped out, guiding his mouth back to hers.

"Yes, ma'am." He chuckled against her lips. "You know, I've wanted this for a long time."

"Me too," she murmured. "So why are we both still talking?

"Good point."

Delaney claimed her lips in a kiss that emptied her mind of all rational thought. All she knew was that she could go on kissing him like this forever. Just when she thought the moment couldn't get any better, he broke contact with her lips to trail kisses along her jaw, dipping lower to press a kiss below her ear and nuzzle the sensitive skin along her throat and collarbone. Her breath was now coming in short little pants that matched his own erratic breathing as he nudged aside the neckline of her sweater.

The moment shattered with the unwelcome peal of a cell phone echoing through the room.

"Hell," Foster groaned. "I have to get that."

"Oh, right." Marina scrambled from the couch, both disappointed and irritated by the interruption.

Another chime rang out, and Foster grunted as he struggled to heft himself from the couch while favoring his injured foot.

"No!" Marina gently pushed him down. "You stay put," she admonished as his cell phone rang out again. "I'll get it for you."

"Thanks." Delaney settled back against the sofa. "It's charging in the kitchen."

As Marina rounded the couch, Delaney seized her hand. "We'll talk more later." He gave her fingers a reassuring squeeze. "There are things we need to work out."

She nodded, inwardly cursing the tenacious *ring-ring* of the cell phone that was preventing them from "working things out" right away. Reluctantly, she tugged her hand free of Delaney's and hurried into the kitchen to find his offending piece of technology.

Ring, ring!

"All right already," Marina grumbled. "I'm coming!" The cell lay face up on the counter, so it wasn't as if she were snooping, but she still felt guilty for stealing a glance at the illuminated screen.

Until she saw the name of the caller displayed there: Deidra Torres.

This was the call Delaney *had* to take?

Suddenly she was thrust back in time, reliving Grayson's betrayal all over again. He'd been in the shower when his cell phone had chirped with an incoming text. Marina wasn't sure what had made her check it that day—she'd never felt the need before—but the message displayed on the screen left little doubt that Grayson had been cheating on her with a woman who worked at his firm.

And now it felt like the betrayal was happening all over again.

Snatches of Deidra's conversation in Argyle's copy room on Wednesday flashed through Marina's head. *He just wanted to get me in his office alone...couldn't keep his eyes off me. He wanted his hands all over me, too. He wants to see me tomorrow after work.* Had Delaney been with Deidra before following her here to Ogunquit?

Marina shut her eyes against the memories and the name currently displayed on the cell's illuminated screen. Thoughts swirled through her head...humiliation, denial, and most of all, anger. She couldn't believe she'd let another man do this to her. Worse than that, she'd let her employer do this to her.

Cursing her stupidity and weakness, Marina ripped Delaney's cell phone from the wall. Marching into the great room, she flung the still ringing cell phone into his lap. "From the looks of it, I'm not the only woman you've got to"—she made air quotes with her fingers—"*work things out with.*"

"What the—?" he started, struggling to get up. As he did so, his injured foot clumsily swung across the coffee table, striking the dolphin figurine.

Marina watched in horror as the delicate sculpture slammed against the metal legs of the end table before crashing to the hardwood floor and breaking into several pieces. "No!" she gasped, her hand flying to her mouth.

Delaney crumpled to the floor with a groan, gathering the pieces of jade dolphin in his palm. "I'm so sorry." He grimaced, his voice thick with remorse. "I'll buy you another one—"

"No." Marina silenced him with a firm shake of her head. Like the shattered pieces of her heart, the dolphin—and everything it represented—was fractured beyond repair. "I'd like Reese to drive me back to Portland tomorrow. Please have him pick me up at noon."

"Marina, wait!" Delaney implored, finally managing to stand up.

Deliberately shutting out the vulnerability of his pleading voice, Marina forced herself not to break into a run as she climbed the stairs. She felt Delaney's eyes following her retreating back and winced when she heard him call out her name again.

But she didn't stop walking until the bedroom door had clicked shut behind her.

Marina's misery felt like a steel weight dragging her to the floor. She huddled there, legs pulled up under her chin, her face pillowed in her arms as waves of humiliation and disappointment washed over her. Gratefully, exhaustion soon claimed her, pulling her down into the black, welcoming void of sleep.

— —

On Sunday morning, Marina awoke with a start.

Gingerly lifting her head, she surveyed the room. But she was quite alone. She must have dreamed the strong arms that had cradled her against a firm chest as she was gently deposited upon the bed, and the butterfly-soft caress that brushed her forehead.

And yet, an almost tangible recollection of Delaney carrying her to bed left lingering doubts in her waking thoughts. As Marina lay there trying to convince herself to get up and face the day, the playful clicks and whistles of dolphins chirped somewhere near her ear.

"Ugh!" she grumbled, rolling onto her side and covering her head with the pillow. Normally, the cheery ringtone brought a smile to her face. But this morning it only served to grate on her frayed nerves.

Reaching for her cell phone, with no more intention than to silence it and let the call ring straight through to voicemail, the name displayed on the screen quickly changed her mind. It was Tony. The poor man had called several times the day before, when she'd forgotten her cell phone, and he'd left several voice mails as well.

Lazily propping the device against her ear, she mumbled a drowsy greeting. "Hey, Tony."

"Marina, honey?" Tony's excited voice vibrated through the speaker. "Lucas came into the restaurant for breakfast this morning. He told me your employer showed up at his cabin looking for you last night. You know, now that I think of it, I bet that really was him you saw at the restaurant on Friday. Anyway..." He rambled on, barely taking a breath between sentences.

"Lucas said your employer was pretty upset to find you at his place, but we can chat about that later. Your yummy lumberjack is pretty worried about you. He said you took off without a word. I told him I'd call and check on you—and I really don't mind—but the man really needs to get a cell phone so he can do these things for himself, you know?"

Marina couldn't argue with that. If he'd had a cell on him last night, it would have been a simple matter to call Eric and have him come pick her up. Then last night's "Delaney Disaster" could have been avoided.

And then there was the fact that If Lucas had a cell phone, she could have called him this morning to thank him for his hospitality and bid him a proper farewell. But circumstances being what they were, she'd have to walk over to his cabin. She just didn't know how she was going to fit it in, on top of everything else. According to the alarm clock on the nightstand, it was already past nine, and she still had to get ready, pack her things, and tidy up her suite so she could leave it as clean as she'd found it upon her arrival.

As if in agreement that there was no time to waste, the bed suddenly released its hold on her. Marina scowled at the comfortable mattress and reluctantly sat up, cautious not to tweak her sore ribs.

"So..." Tony hesitated meaningfully. "Are you all right, hon?"

"It's a long story," she sighed, swinging her legs over the side of the bed. "And I'd really like to tell you about it, but I'm heading back to Portland at noon, and I have so much to do before—"

"You're leaving?" he squawked. "What about the rest of your vacation? And we still need to discuss the wedding venues I looked into. Did you get my messages?"

"I did. I'm sorry I didn't call back," Marina said regretfully. "But I didn't have my phone with me yesterday, and, well, as you can imagine, it was quite an eventful day."

"Ooh, that's a story I'm dying to hear," he cooed dramatically, but his voice held a note of disappointment. "I guess it'll just have to wait for another time. I just wish you weren't going so soon. Jake and I were hoping to have you over for dinner at our place."

"I would've loved that, Tony. But..." She paused, a vivid reminder of exactly *why* she had to leave Ogunquit playing through her mind. "I really can't talk about it right now," Marina sniffled.

She could almost hear Tony pursing his lips, almost feel his indignation through the phone. "I don't know what your employer did to you. But if I ever get my hands on him, I'll rip off his man ornament and feed it to Armani."

Marina snorted through her sniffles. "Thanks. I needed a good laugh."

"You're welcome," he answered earnestly. "But I wasn't joking."

"I know." She smiled, warmed by the protective-older-brother tone in his voice. "Listen, I've got to jump in the shower, but I'll call you later today, after I've had a chance to unpack and get settled in at home."

"OK, but if I don't hear from you," he warned, "I'll be calling you to get the play-by-play on boss-lover's little impromptu visit!"

"Talk to you this afternoon." Marina shook her head at Tony's histrionics. But at least she was smiling as she padded into the bathroom, despite the heavy weight of Delaney's betrayal upon her heart.

— ~

When Marina finally shuffled downstairs to start a pot of coffee, it was nearly ten thirty.

She heaved a sigh of relief that Delaney was nowhere in sight. With any luck, he would remain ensconced somewhere in the bowels of the cabin until her departure at noon.

Absently going through the motions of extracting a mug from the cupboard and cream from the fridge, Marina lamented the late hour. She knew there wouldn't be enough time to walk over to Lucas's place before Reese picked her up. She'd attempted to pack, but her hungry stomach had protested, luring her downstairs for some breakfast. Needless to say, her clothes still lay in a heap in her open suitcase. And she hadn't managed to do any cleaning either.

As she sipped her coffee, Marina felt a little twitch of guilt in her stomach. It wouldn't be right to leave without thanking Lucas for his kindness and hospitality, especially after the way she'd walked out on him last night. She made a mental note to ask Reese if they could make a short stop at Lucas's cabin before heading back to Portland.

She nibbled at her lip as another thought occurred to her. She couldn't remember thanking Delaney for the care and concern he'd shown her after her accident. Regardless of his betrayal, he still deserved her gratitude for the way he'd seen to her care in her concussed state. She just didn't know how she was going to face him after what had passed between them last night.

Marina was startled from her thoughts as the doorbell chimed three times in rapid succession, reverberating throughout the cabin's interior. Casting a glance at the time displayed on the microwave, she frowned. Reese wasn't due until noon. Was Delaney expecting someone? Shuffling from the kitchen, she expected to see her employer limping for the door. When he didn't emerge, she fleetingly wondered if his ankle felt worse this morning and if he might be in need of her assistance.

"Seriously?" she muttered aloud. "Foster Delaney doesn't need anything from *you*." The realization sent a fresh wave of bitterness through her, and she yanked the door open with more force than she'd intended, wincing at the sharp pinch to her ribs. Marina's grimace of pain melted away the instant her eyes connected with those of the unexpected visitor.

And then she was collapsing into his arms.

16

"**E**rik!" Marina exclaimed, hugging her closest friend as if she hadn't seen him in ages even though it had only been days. "What are you doing here?"

"It's nice to see you, too."

She heard the familiar smirk in his voice and thought she'd never heard anything so wonderful in her life.

"So, interesting story..." Erik pulled away from her slightly. "I had a feeling something was wrong when the ole gypsy intuition woke me out of a dead sleep this morning. Then, right after that, I got this cryptic text message on my cell phone with directions to pick you up here and drive you back to Portland."

Marina frowned. Delaney surprised her at every turn, toying with her affections one moment, and arranging for her dearest friend to drive her home the next. Admittedly, though, she was grudgingly appreciative of his thoughtfulness.

"What's happened?" Erik asked as Marina ushered him inside. "Are you all right?"

"Long story." She shrugged. "Oh, and just a heads up, the ole gypsy intuition needs a serious tune-up. It's off by a few days."

"Why?" He cocked a black brow at her. "What happened a few days ago?"

"I'll tell you all about it on the way home," she promised. "But I'd rather not stick around here any longer than I have to."

Apparently, her employer shared her sentiment. "How soon can I expect the two of you to be on your way?" his clipped tones drifted into the foyer from the hall.

Marina bristled at Delaney's words. If he wanted her gone, then fine. But Erik didn't deserve his rudeness. After all, he'd driven all the way up to Ogunquit at his employer's request.

Erik placed a calming hand on her shoulder and gave it a quick squeeze before addressing Delaney. "Since I can only assume that *you* were the one who sent me the text message about picking Rina up here, I'll let you tell me what you have in mind, *boss*."

A muscle jumped in Delaney's cheek at the sarcasm in Erik's response as he limped into the foyer, brushing past Marina without a glance. "Originally Reese was scheduled to pick Marina up at noon. But I have an appointment here at twelve thirty that I need to make some preparations for, so I'd appreciate it if you could be gone by eleven forty-five."

Delaney was freshly showered and dressed in a crisp gray shirt and black slacks, the clean woodsy scent of him wreaking havoc on Marina's senses, despite her annoyance with him. She barely managed to paste a bland expression on her face. "That shouldn't be a problem," she replied curtly, even as she surveyed his injured foot and faltering steps with a reluctant twinge of sympathy.

"Will you excuse us?" She fluttered her fingers in a dismissive wave, hoping he'd take the hint and leave before she lost her composure.

With an almost imperceptible flinch of his jaw, Delaney turned his back on them and shuffled down the dim hallway.

"What's his problem?" Erik inquired, his thumb jabbing at the space Delaney had just vacated.

"Can we talk about this later?" she pleaded, her voice quavering. It had taken a force of will to pretend indifference to Delaney's callousness, and she didn't know how much longer she could keep her emotions in check.

"All right." Erik shrugged. "Are your things ready?"

"Oh, uh…not quite. Give me twenty minutes?" It wouldn't give her much time to clean and straighten her room the way she'd like to, but that couldn't be helped now.

"Well, get to it, Rina-girl." He swatted her playfully, his gaze darting over her left shoulder. "Got anything good to eat in this chateau royale?"

"The kitchen's loaded." Marina laughed, sweeping her hand in open invitation. "Help yourself."

"I think I will." He waggled his eyebrows, ducking around her.

She shook her head, staring after him in fond amusement as she turned to climb the stairs. Before she could take even one step, though, the doorbell chimed out the arrival of a second visitor. Marina spun around just as a scowling Delaney reemerged from the hallway.

"Expecting any uninvited guests?" he muttered, hobbling past her to answer the door. "What the hell are you doing here?" Delaney hissed at the new visitor.

Marina gasped at his unnecessary rudeness, but she understood what had provoked him when she heard Lucas's voice drift into the foyer.

"I'd like to speak with Marina, please," he drawled.

"Conveniently developed manners overnight, have you?" Delaney retorted.

"Always had 'em," Lucas countered. "It just didn't occur to me to use 'em on an arrogant son of a—" His words were cut off by a keening animal whine as Hawk suddenly shot through the door.

Delaney stumbled out of the way, almost toppling over, as the dog flew past him and made a beeline for Marina. "Get your animal out of my house!" he roared at Lucas, who vaulted through the door after Hawk.

"*Your* house?" Marina tilted her head in question. Since the day she'd arrived at the cabin, a niggling suspicion that it actually belonged to Delaney had started to make more and more sense to her. She couldn't say why, exactly, but something about the energy of the place made it feel like more than a rental.

"Well, uh...yeah," Delaney stumbled over his words. "You know, it's my, uh...temporary home, just as it's been yours... while on vacation, I mean."

She studied him curiously for a moment then shrugged it off, distracted by Hawk's excited whimpers and the wet lap of his tongue across the back of her hand.

"Hello, boy!" Marina rubbed the top of his head, threading her fingers through the thick fur at his neck as she looked up to greet his owner. "Good morning, Lucas."

"Mornin'." He bobbed his head and smiled. "How're you feelin'?"

"This thing is coming along nicely." She tapped her head with one finger. "The ribs aren't too happy to be up and moving, though."

"Yep, they're probably gonna be ornery for a while yet." Lucas nodded, scrubbing a hand through his hair. "You left without sayin' good-bye last night."

"I know, and I'm so sorry." She reached out to place a hand on his arm. "I meant to stop by your place this morning."

"Ahem." Delaney cleared his throat.

Lucas ignored him, his eyes fixed on Marina. "So you're not upset with me then?"

"Of course not." She smiled reassuringly. "I'm so glad you dropped by."

"In that case, so am I." A blinding-white grin split across his handsome face. "Hawk is, too, aren't ya boy?"

The dog woofed happily, his tail thumping enthusiastically against the shiny wood floor.

"Hawk can't seem to get enough of this place." Lucas chortled, hooking one thumb in his jeans, the other poking in the direction of the deck. "First the hot tub, now the inner sanctum."

"Your dog was in my hot tub?" Delaney huffed in disgust.

Just as Lucas opened his mouth to make what Marina knew would have been another sarcastic comeback, Erik emerged from the kitchen with his hand in a bag of potato chips, his gaze narrowing on the newcomers.

"Erik, come meet Lucas and Hawk." Marina nodded at her pair of friends, doing her best to ignore Delaney's glowering expression.

He wiped his hand on his jeans and thrust it at Lucas. "Hey, man."

Lucas gave Erik a man nod and a robust hand shake.

"Is that your doing?" Erik flicked his head at Marina, whose hand stroked lazy circles in the thick coat at Hawk's neck.

"Nope." Lucas shook his head. "I just supplied the dog. She did the rest."

"Oh, I think you deserve a lot more credit than that," Marina quickly interjected.

Erik considered Lucas with an expression of grudging respect. "Well, whatever you did, you helped her accomplish what I couldn't, even with the help of my gypsy—"

"Excuse me," Delaney interrupted icily, leveling his cold, green glare on Lucas. "Your dog is still in *my* house."

"So is the flashlight I loaned you last night," Lucas shot back. "But you don't hear me gripin' about it."

"Why should you?" Delaney scoffed. "It's a piece of junk that can't generate enough power to light the inside of a matchbox."

Erik's gaze bounced expectantly between Lucas and Delaney, his features registering the excitement of a man anticipating a good fight.

Marina was almost sorry to disappoint him. But she couldn't stand another minute of Delaney's attitude or his treatment of her friends. Before Lucas could respond to her employer's jibe, she pulled him aside. "Would you and Hawk mind waiting for me out on the deck?" she asked, lightly touching his arm. "I'll be out in just a minute."

For a moment, it looked as if Lucas would ignore her request in favor of flinging another round of verbal insults at Delaney. But after a prolonged hesitation, during which his brown eyes took on a mischievous gleam, he pulled her against him in an affectionate hug.

"Sure thing, darlin'." Casting a taunting glance at Delaney, he motioned for Hawk to follow him. "How about another swim in the nice man's hot tub while we wait for Marina? Eh, boy?"

Striding through the dining area, Lucas exited the sliding-glass doors with Hawk and Erik trailing behind him. With a resigned sigh, Marina turned to confront her employer.

"What happened between us last night has nothing to do with my friends, so stop being such a jerk to them." She poked a finger at his unyielding chest and immediately wished she hadn't. Memories of being crushed against him jolted through her.

Delaney must have recognized the change in her, because he closed his fingers over hers, flattening them against his chest. "Marina..." His voice was a desperate whisper. "That call from Deidra...it's not what you think."

Gazing into the emerald pools of his eyes, Marina searched for hints of another lie. She felt her resolve weakening, could almost hear the ice around her heart cracking. Then she was leaning into him, her lips only a breath away from his.

Then the moment shattered with another peal of the doorbell.

"Damn it," Delaney growled, reluctantly releasing Marina's hand. "It's like Grand Central Station around here," he muttered, shuffling to the door.

Marina's head swirled with conflicted thoughts. The earnest expression on Delaney's face just now had seemed so authentic, his voice so sincere. But could she trust it?

She came hurtling back to reality when she heard the cloying voice of a woman she'd never expected to encounter on her vacation in Ogunquit.

Deidra Torres.

Fisting her hands on her curvy hips, Deidra stared down her perfect nose at Marina. "What is *she* doing here?" the woman demanded petulantly, leveling her narrow-eyed, amber gaze on Delaney.

"Funny, I was just about to ask you the same thing," Marina remarked offhandedly, noticing the way Delaney swiped at the sheen of perspiration on his forehead. "But that's a moot point now."

Marina struggled to keep her expression impassive, but her voice held an accusing tone when she finally composed herself enough to address Delaney. "Looks like your twelve-thirty appointment arrived early."

His agitated gaze snapped from the pouting Deidra back to Marina. "She isn't..." He took a step toward her, holding out his hands imploringly. "It's not—" Delaney tried again.

But Marina was done listening to his lies.

"He's all yours, Deidra." Turning her back on them, Marina slowly left the room, shutting the sliding glass doors behind her with an air of finality.

17

"What's wrong?" Erik gaped at Marina. "You look like you want to murder someone."

"*Two* someones, actually," she replied through stiff lips. "Deidra Torres just joined the party."

"Deidra Torres, from Argyle?" Erik's face scrunched into a bewildered frown. "What the hell?"

"Exactly," she muttered, folding her arms around her middle.

"Who's Deidra Torres?" Lucas looked from Marina to Erik and back again.

"Oh, sorry." Marina grimaced. "She's the employee I told you I saw leaving Delaney's office on Wednesday as I was going in to be informed of this mandatory vacation." She swept her arm toward the cabin.

"Hmmm." Lucas drew his lips in thoughtfully, scrubbing a hand over his face. "I guess I was wrong about the man's intentions."

"You're not just saying that because you want to hook up with me, are you?" Marina flashed him a saucy grin.

Soda sputtered from Erik's mouth, and he swiped it away with the sleeve of his shirt.

"Take it easy, ole man." Lucas clapped Erik on the back.

"Do I need to give you two some privacy?" Erik's questioning gaze slid back and forth between them.

"Don't be ridiculous!" Marina snorted at the same time Lucas quipped, "You won't hear me objectin'."

There was a sudden shift in Erik's mood, his brows furrowing as he studied her face. "Wait a sec. You're not thinking the twelve-thirty appointment Delaney was referring to was actually supposed to be Deidra, are you?"

"It did cross my mind." Marina scraped her teeth against her lower lip.

"I know what it looks like, but it doesn't make any sense." Erik shook his head, pointing one brown index finger at the cabin. "I'm pretty sure Delaney doesn't care much for that woman. And besides, if he was going to invite a second woman up here, wouldn't he give himself more time than forty-five minutes to make good and sure the first one was long gone before the next one showed up?"

"Hmmm." Lucas nodded, pursing his lips. "You make a good point."

"But why would she just show up here out of the blue?" Marina rubbed her temples. "The only thing that makes sense to me is that Delaney invited her."

"Also a valid point." Lucas scratched his chin.

Erik shot him an irritated look. "Is that all you have to say?"

"How about...Delaney's a bonehead?" Lucas shrugged and cast Marina an overly solicitous grin.

She would've laughed, but the corners of her mouth felt as if they were attached to the heavy weight tugging at her heart, and she barely managed a feeble half-smile in return.

"Come on, Marina." Erik placed a protective arm around her shoulders. "I think we should get you out of here."

"I need to say good-bye to Lucas and Hawk first."

"OK." Erik swigged the last of his soda and crushed the can between his palms. "While you're doing that, I'll get your luggage loaded into the car."

"There are still a few things on the bed that need to be thrown in the suitcase."

"Got it," Erik acknowledged. "Meet you out front in a few minutes." Shaking hands with Lucas, the two men exchanged nods, and Erik disappeared into the house.

— —

"It's shame." Lucas cast a rueful look at Marina. "You leavin' like this, with four days of vacation left."

"Yes, well...I hadn't counted on it turning into such a mess." Admittedly, she'd had a funny feeling about the gratis vacation from the start. But she could not completely regret coming to Ogunquit when she considered the new friendships that had come out of it.

"I'd really like to keep in touch through e-mail, and..." Marina nibbled at her bottom lip, surprised to find that it was trembling. She'd grown genuinely fond of Lucas in the short time she'd known him. "I'd like you and Hawk to come visit me in Portland when you get a chance." Marina scanned the backyard. "Where is he, anyway?"

"Out explorin', I guess." He shrugged. "But if I call him now, he'll just monopolize you in the few minutes we have left to say good-bye." Lucas shoved his hands into the pockets of his jeans. After a lengthy pause, his expression brightened. "Hey, I was wonderin' if you'd mind me using your experiences with bonehead in there"—his head bobbed toward the cabin—"as the premise for my next book?"

"Hmmm." Marina pursed her lips, one index finger tapping her chin. "Only if you promise to send me the first published copy."

"Of course." Lucas beamed.

"Any ideas what you'll name this novel of yours?"

"I was thinkin' of *Cabin Fever*."

"Or you could call it *Ditching Delaney*," Marina quipped with a wry smile.

"Too close to home for you, I think." Lucas shook his head. Suddenly, his face creased with a sly grin. "How about...*Blowing off Bonehead*?"

"That would work." She grimaced, her wistful gaze sliding to the cabin behind them.

"I'm sorry he hurt you, Marina." Lucas curved one long finger under her chin, lifting her face to meet his sympathetic gaze. "I wish I could take away the pain."

"I can think of something that might help," she replied hesitantly.

He quirked a brow at her. "I'm listening."

"I could use a hug." Marina whispered.

Lucas didn't hesitate to wrap his big arms around her, pulling her close. Marina relaxed in his embrace, nestling her cheek against the hard warmth of his flannel-covered chest. Once again, she wished she'd met Lucas before her feelings for Delaney had thoroughly made a mess of her heart.

"Don't go." Lucas crushed her closer. "Spend the rest of your vacation with me."

"As tempting as that is…" Marina shook her head against his chest. "You know I can't."

They stood there, holding each other for several long moments. Finally, with a reluctant sigh, she pulled back and reached up to cup his face in her hand. "I can't thank you enough." She swallowed past the lump developing in her throat. "Last night, you were such a comfort to me."

"You know"— he smiled down at her, still holding her in his embrace— "as a romance writer, I'm always rescuin' damsels in distress through my characters." Amusement twinkled in the depths of his earth-colored eyes. "It was kinda nice to actually do it for real this time."

"I'd say you come by it quite naturally." Marina regarded him thoughtfully. "Let's see…" She began to tick off his virtues on her fingers. "You're an author, a skilled dog-paranoia therapist, an excellent hot chocolate maker…Is there anything you can't do?"

"Yeah," Lucas snorted. "Apparently I can't kiss well enough to get the girl."

"There's nothing wrong with your kissing." Marina felt her cheeks flood with heat, recalling the pleasant brush of his lips on hers, and the undercurrent of restrained passion. She didn't doubt this man's ability to thoroughly melt a woman's bones. Unfortunately her heart and head had been otherwise occupied. "Maybe I'm just not the *right* girl."

"Would you care to test that theory?" A wicked grin tugged at the corners of his sensuous mouth. "I mean, now that your bonehead boss has totally screwed things up, you might feel differently about my, uh... skills."

"You're shameless." Marina rolled her eyes. "Still...I think you've more than earned a good-bye kiss."

"Hey, I'll take what I can get." Lucas ducked his head and covered her mouth with his.

His kiss was gentle at first. But then she felt him smile against her lips as he deepened the kiss, one hand slipping down to cover her bottom and tug her against the hard contours of his body.

Marina was the first to break off the kiss. "You did that on purpose!" She swatted at him playfully.

"Guilty." Lucas chuckled, nodding at the cabin. "Just in case someone happened to be watchin'."

Suddenly, a third body, warm and furry, leaped upon them, pawing and mewling.

"Hawk, down!" Lucas grumbled, trying to push the dog away. "I'm not done sayin' good-bye to Marina yet."

"Oh yes you are." Marina slipped out of Lucas's arms to embrace the excited dog. "You've had your good-bye kiss, mister. It's Hawk's turn now." She dropped a smooch on the dog's wet nose.

"He's really gonna miss you, Marina." The amused lilt in his voice had disappeared. "We both will. Are you sure you won't change your mind and stay a few more days?"

"Under different circumstances—"

"Okay, I get it," Lucas cut her off, shoving his hands into his pockets. "Hawk, tell Marina good-bye."

She knelt down and wrapped her arms around the dog. "I want you to come visit me in Portland—OK, boy?" Pulling away, she scratched behind his ears. "I have an idiotic cat there you can chase around." A low growl rumbled in Hawk's throat, and Marina smiled. "I thought you might like that."

Standing, she turned to face Lucas. But when she opened her mouth to say good-bye, he smothered the words with a lingering kiss.

When Marina opened her eyes, he had backed away.

"Hawk, come!" he commanded the whining canine.

But the dog simply cocked his head, eyes darting uncertainly between Marina and his owner. "Go on, boy," she urged the dog, patting his hind quarters.

Suppressing a melancholy sigh, she watched her friends disappear through the trees as she descended the deck stairs. Heading around to the front of the house, she stopped and peered around, feeling as if a pair of eyes watched her. Shaking it off, she approached Erik's black Nissan Maxima idling in the drive.

But Erik was nowhere in sight.

— ◡ —

Thinking Erik had probably run back into the cabin for some reason or another, Marina settled into the front passenger seat to wait. She pushed the automatic control buttons on the passenger side door, cracking open her window a few inches to let in the spicy redolence of Ogunquit's crisp autumn air.

That's when she caught a sudden movement out of the corner of her eye. Glancing up, she let out a squeak of surprise, her hand flying to her chest.

"Marina, you can't go like this!" Delaney shouted, pounding his fist on the window. "We need to talk!"

"Actions speak louder than words, Delaney." she flung back. "And I've seen more than enough action!"

"Oh, that's rich coming from the woman who was kissing me last night and making out with another man this morning!"

So she hadn't imagined the feeling of being watched after all. "Y-you were spying on me?"

"It's not spying if it happens on your own—" He stopped midsentence, swiping a hand over his jaw.

"Your own property?" Marina shot back. "Is that what you've been trying so hard *not* to say? Why would you even hide that from me?"

Delaney's gaze flicked to the cabin as he braced his hands on the car's hood above her window. "I thought it might make you feel uncomfortable if you knew."

"I'll tell you what makes me uncomfortable"—she nearly slammed her hand against the dashboard as she thrust it in the direction of the cabin—"Deidra Torres apparently knew about it before I did. Am I the only woman in the office who *didn't* get the memo?"

"No!" Delaney slapped the roof of the car with his hand. "I have no idea why Deidra showed up here!"

His desperate assertion stirred up bitter memories as Grayson's words slammed into her head. *"I have no idea why that woman's calling me!"* Marina clamped her hands over her ears as if it could somehow silence the echo of Grayson's voice inside her head. Did all men feed women with the same lies? And were all women as gullible as she'd been? Well, just because she'd believed it more than once, didn't mean she had to fall for it again.

Refusing to look at Delaney, Marina's hand hovered over the automatic window control on her door handle, but she was too late. He curled his fingers over the lip of the window, his knuckles turning white as he bore down.

Delaney leaned so close to the window she could feel the warm huff of his breath. "I know how messed up this looks, but I can explain. Please, Marina. Talk to me."

Marina shut her eyes so she wouldn't be tempted to look at him. Unfortunately, he wasn't making it easy for her to tune him out.

"Damn it, Marina!" Delaney ripped out the words with a frustrated growl, his hands shaking the window they still gripped. "You're not being fair!"

"Back off, Delaney."

Marina expelled a relieved breath when she heard Erik's voice. Despite his propensity to be a shameless tease on most days, he was also fiercely protective. Whenever she found herself in a real pinch, she could always count on him to rescue her, whether she was being accosted by vicious Pomeranians or maniacal employers.

"Marina's had a rough day," her avenging angel was saying. "Don't make it any worse. You're going to have to cool the hell down before I let you talk to her again, savvy?"

What? Marina couldn't believe her ears. What was Erik thinking? She had no plans to resume this conversation with Delaney. *Ever!* Determined to take matters into her own hands before her presumptuous hero started discussing the terms of her surrender, she leaned closer to his window. "Get. In!" she hissed.

Obediently, Erik slunk into the driver's seat just as Delaney's desperate voice reverberated through the car's interior. "Just give me a few minutes, Marina. *Please.*"

Turning back to her employer, Marina ignored the pleading look in his enigmatic green eyes. She couldn't afford to be distracted by the bleakness of his expression. For all she knew, it wasn't even real. Just like everything he'd told her.

Lifting her chin, Marina forced her lips to move. "You were the one who couldn't wait to see us gone, and now you want to get all chatty? I don't think so. Now move away from the car before I have Erik run over the foot you're not limping on."

Erik choked back a bark of laughter as she rolled up her window and focused her attention on the front windshield.

After a long pause, Erik pointed a brown finger at her window. "You know he's still standing there, right?"

"Yeah, I know." Marina continued to stare straight ahead. "Can we please just get out of here?"

With a reluctant sigh, Erik shifted the car into gear but didn't pull forward. "Are you sure?"

"I'm sure." In the rearview mirror, Marina watched as Delaney finally turned his back on them and hobbled back to the cabin, where Deidra Torres waited for him on the front porch.

18

"How's Her Majesty?" Marina asked as Erik merged onto I-95 North.

"How do you think?" He slanted her an amused grin.

"Quite content to rule the roost without me, I imagine," she replied with a self-deprecating puff of laughter as she watched the scenery fly by. At this speed, they'd make the forty-five-minute drive back to Portland in less than half an hour. "How did you and Mr. Hiroshi get on in my absence?"

"The man thinks I'm his best friend now." He smirked. "He calls me every day to discuss professional baseball. Or, at least, I think that's what he's talking about. I don't speak Japanese, so it's kind of hard to tell. He could just as easily be cussing me out."

"My money's on the cussing." Marina snorted, her eyes shifting to the photo of Erik's fiancée encased in a plastic frame attached to the dashboard. "Didn't Jill want to come?"

"Yeah, she loves it down here." Erik nodded in acknowledgment. "She was pretty ticked that her stomach was still churning this morning."

Marina looked at him askance. "This has been going on for at least two weeks. Maybe she should go see a doctor."

"She already has." A secretive smile played about his lips.

Marina's eyes widened. "You mean...?"

"Yeah." His smile turned up a notch. "We're about seven weeks along."

"That's wonderful!" She squealed with delight, lunging awkwardly across the center console to throw her arm around his neck and kiss his cheek.

"Wow." Erik chuckled when the Maxima swerved slightly under her assault. "You're really that excited about being a babysitter, huh?"

"Ha-ha." Marina winced as she eased back into her seat.

"All right, spill it." His gaze narrowed at her discomfort, his dark eyes dropping to where her hand was wrapped around her torso. "What happened, Rina?"

For the next twenty minutes, she related everything that had occurred since arriving in Ogunquit. He scowled when she'd narrated the events leading up to Deidra's call and subsequent arrival at the vacation rental and howled with laughter when she told him how Lucas had thrown Delaney out of his cabin and he'd sprained his ankle.

"So that's why he was limping!" he guffawed, slapping the steering wheel with his hand. "He totally deserved that."

As Erik surveyed the road ahead, his expressive face suddenly became somber. "Maybe you were right all along...about my gypsy intuition, I mean." He expelled an audible breath. "Even I'm starting to wonder if it's not a load of crap."

Her eyes widened at his confession. She knew how hard it was for Erik to admit such a thing at the cost of his Romany pride. "What makes you say that?" she urged softly.

"Well, for starters, this whole Deidra thing doesn't bode well for Delaney's character. I had him pegged as a real decent sort of guy."

She stared at him, baffled. "Then why were you taking his side back there...promising I'd talk to him when he cooled down?"

Erik shrugged. "I guess, deep down, there's a stubborn part of me that's still clinging to the belief that he's a good guy who just made a stupid mistake, you know? And..." He grabbed her hand and gave it a meaningful squeeze. "I wanted to make sure you didn't burn all your bridges, just in case there was a chance that it could still work out between you two."

"Thanks, but there's no chance." With a heavy sigh, Marina sagged against the headrest. "But none of this implies that your gypsy intuition is crap. You said before you got the text message to come get me this morning that you had a feeling something was wrong," she reminded him.

"Yeah, well...that could've been a fluke." He shrugged. "Besides, Delaney wasn't the only thing I may have been wrong about." His expression was grim as he watched her. "Milo and Suki broke up."

"Oh no," Marina gasped, her hand coming up to cover her mouth. She felt a sharp pang of sympathy for Suki, knowing how much her friend had liked their coworker. "What happened?"

Erik shook his head, eyes on the road as he exited the highway into Portland. "I don't know all the details. Only that Suki said he's not the same person anymore, that he's been acting strange lately."

Her mind shot back to the company party in May, when she'd seen him arguing with Deidra. And last Wednesday night, she'd glimpsed Milo watching her as she boarded the elevator at Argyle. Marina wasn't sure what to make of either instance, but it wasn't Milo she was worried about at the moment. "How's Suki doing?"

"She's understandably heartbroken." Erik grimaced. "And I feel like it's my fault."

"I'm sure Suki doesn't blame you," Marina reassured him as they pulled into the parking spot nearest her condo building. "And neither should—" The words died on her lips when she caught sight of the man exiting the renovated Victorian structure she called home.

It was her ex, Grayson Munro.

"What the hell is he doing here?" Erik bit out the words through clenched teeth.

"I don't know, but I think he saw us." Marina cursed as she watched Grayson head in their direction. "Judging by the determined look on his face, I don't think I'm likely to escape this *happy* little reunion."

"Well, I'm not leaving you alone with that prick," Erik warned, his narrow-eyed gaze focused on her approaching ex.

"I was hoping you'd say that." Marina smiled gratefully. "Why don't you hang out in the kitchen or guest room and give Jill the play-by-play while I talk to him?"

A wicked grin tugged at Erik's mouth. "She's going to love this."

After insisting on carrying Marina's luggage up to her second-floor condo, Grayson fawned over Her Majesty and complimented Marina on how tidy her home looked. Then, after grudgingly coming to terms with the fact that Erik wasn't about to leave them alone, Grayson settled on her sofa, where he now patted the empty cushion beside him, his steel-gray eyes glinting with undisguised invitation.

Marina ignored it. "What are you doing here, Grayson?" she asked blandly, crossing her arms over her chest. From the corner of her eye, she could see Erik, cell phone pressed to his ear, giving her the thumbs-up from his hiding place in the kitchen, and she struggled to suppress a smile.

"Oh, come on, Mare..." Grayson purred out the nickname he'd bestowed upon her a few months into their relationship. "Sit with me." He patted the cushion next to him more vigorously then draped his arm over the back of the couch.

Marina winced. "Don't call me that." She cast a helpless glance at Erik who mirrored her sentiment with a silent gagging motion. Why Grayson thought he could waltz back into her life and call her by the pet name she'd never much cared for, she'd never understand. And she was too exhausted to deal with his nonsense anyway. "Listen, I'm really tired, and I still have to unpack, so—"

"Aren't you even going to listen to what I have to say?" he asked glumly. "I've been trying to call, but you never pick up."

"Why should I, Grayson?" she shot back, her irritation mounting. "I haven't heard from you in, I don't know, eight months now? What could you possibly have to say that you think I'd want to hear?"

"That I'm sorry?"

Marina wavered, scarcely able to believe Grayson Munro had actually apologized. And when he stood and crossed over to her with outstretched arms, she was so completely taken off guard she didn't even shrug off his hands when they curled around her shoulders with a possessive grip. She'd almost forgotten how devastatingly handsome he could be when he used the full force of his charms on her.

"I realize I haven't been in touch, but don't take my absence the wrong way. I know how much your sister meant to you, and...well, I just wanted to give you the necessary time to mourn her passing."

She heard a stifled snort from the kitchen, and her eyes snapped over to Erik.

Can you believe this guy? he mouthed.

Marina immediately snapped back to her senses. "How generous of you," she muttered, squirming out of his grasp.

But her sarcasm was lost on him. The idiot actually smiled in triumph. "That's my girl. I knew you'd understand."

The absurdness of his response, coupled with the magnitude of his arrogance, sparked Marina's indignation. She should have known the man was incapable of remorse, especially where his own guilt or wrongdoing was concerned.

Stalking over to the door, she swung it open wide. "Get out."

"You can't mean that," Grayson scoffed, eyeing her disbelievingly. "I'm offering to take you back!"

"I don't recall asking you to." Marina fisted her hands on her hips. "Now please leave."

But he simply stood there gawking at her as if he expected her to change her mind. She was just beginning to wonder whether Erik still watched them from the kitchen when her friend noiselessly appeared at Grayson's side.

"Do you need some help finding your way out?" Erik smirked, his tone amused, but his meaning crystal clear.

"Are you going to let him talk to me like that?" Grayson blustered like a petulant four-year-old, pointing an accusing finger in Erik's face.

Marina rolled her eyes. "Yep."

Grayson thrust his face close to hers, glaring at her with reproachful eyes. "You're making the biggest mistake of your life!" he spat out the words contemptuously.

She lifted her chin and met his withering stare with one of her own. "That's a risk I'm willing to live with."

Leveling them with a spiteful glare, Grayson muttered a scathing curse and stormed out the door.

"Wow." Erik let out a low whistle, kicking the door shut behind her ex. "That guy's still a total douche bag."

"Yeah, he is." Marina exhaled, slumping upon the couch. Erik plopped down next to her, Her Majesty leaping up to settle on his lap. *Typical*, she smirked. The animal probably hadn't even noticed, let alone cared, that she'd been gone. "What I don't get is...why, after all this time, both Grayson *and* my parents have suddenly decided to reach out to me."

"Your parents called?" he eyed her thoughtfully. "What did they have to say?"

"I didn't answer it," she admitted hollowly. "I let it go to voice mail."

"Are you going to call them back?"

Before Marina could answer, the cell phone in her jeans pocket chirped out a vibrant chorus of dolphin clicks and whistles.

"Haven't you changed that hideous ringtone yet?" Erik teased, his previous inquiry forgotten. "I feel like I'm at Sea World."

Elbowing her friend in the ribs, she extracted the device from her pocket, blinking in surprise. Why was Tony calling? It was still early yet. She hadn't even had a chance to unpack and settle in, thanks to Grayson's unanticipated visit.

Click, click, whistle, click, click! Her cell phone chimed again and again.

"Are you going to answer that?" Erik plucked the cell from her hand, one dark brow flicking up. "Who's Tony?"

"Your new wedding planner." She made a face at him and snatched the phone back. Punching the receive call button, she held the device to her ear. "Hey, Tony. I was going to call you later, I swear!"

"I believe you, hon." His tone was light, but Marina sensed the underlying restraint. "But that's not why I called."

"Oh?" She tilted her head, tugging at the lobe of her free ear.

"Sweetie, there's something you need to know."

A sick sort of feeling began to swim in the pit of Marina's stomach as she listened to Tony relate how he'd arrived at Delaney's rental cabin in Ogunquit, just half an hour after she and Erik had left.

For a twelve-thirty appointment.

Her heart lurched, matching the sudden chaos in her stomach, as comprehension dawned.

Delaney had been telling the truth.

Erik nudged her open mouth closed with the crook of his finger, whispering that he was heading to the kitchen to rummage for food. She nodded, only half aware of what he'd said, her mind preoccupied with guilt over wrongfully assuming Delaney's appointment had been nothing more than a smoke screen to cover a dalliance with Deidra Torres.

And there was something else bothering her. "So...why did Delaney want to meet with you?"

"Do you remember our conversation at lunch the other day?" Tony's voice went up an octave or two. "The one about me helping a man purchase a home five or six months ago, for a woman who's unaware of his feelings for her?"

The urgency in Tony's voice gave her pause. "Um, yeah..." She rubbed at her forehead.

"Well, honey," he gushed dramatically, "that woman is you!"

She could not possibly have heard him correctly.

That was Marina's first thought. Her second was that Tony had indulged in one cocktail too many. Last, and most bewildering, was the fact that there was no way he could know such a thing. She'd never divulged her employer's name to him, and Delaney was unaware of her acquaintance with Tony.

"Marina?" His voice sounded tinny and distant amidst the maelstrom of thoughts ravaging her head. "You still there, honey?"

"I'm h-here," she answered unsteadily. "But Tony, you must be mistaken."

"Oh, it's no mistake, sweetie," he assured her excitedly. "It's destiny. Listen to this..."

19

Marina would have collapsed upon the floor had the sofa not already been securely beneath her.

While Delaney had admitted to her that he was, in fact, the owner of the cabin in Ogunquit, she was floored by the knowledge that he'd bought it exclusively for *her*. If they hadn't argued last night, the details of the cabin's purchase might have been forthcoming. The fact that she hadn't been aware of the truth until after everything had turned into a colossal mess in no way assuaged her self-reproach for the accusations she'd flung at him.

Erik settled next to her with a heaping bowl of cold cereal and a gallon of milk. "You look a little shell-shocked. What's up?"

"Oh, Erik," she groaned, dropping her head into her hands. "I've been so wrong."

"Hey now, what's this?" he asked, depositing the cereal and milk on the coffee table so he could gather her in his arms.

"Your gypsy magic isn't total crap." She sniffled against his chest. "You were right all along."

"I'm surprised you'd say so." His chuckle was a dry, cynical sound. "After everything that occurred this morning."

"That's just it." She murmured, pulling out of his embrace to look up at him. "We weren't around to see what happened next."

"Ooh, snacks *and* story time!" Erik rubbed his hands together glee-fully, reaching for his cereal and splashing some milk into the bowl.

Marina shook her head, regarding her friend with amusement. Erik was such a big kid sometimes. And before long, Jill was going to have another one to deal with. The poor woman would have her hands full trying to feed and care for them both.

"I'm all ears." He shoveled a spoonful of Fruity Pebbles into his mouth, arching his brows expectantly.

With a subdued sigh, Marina proceeded to tell him everything Tony had said. When she'd finished, Erik looked as shell-shocked as she felt.

"So you're telling me that this Tony guy found the chauffeur's paper on the ground—the one with the rental information and your name and address scribbled on it—and figured out the connection between you and Delaney, which he then used to cleverly manipulate the man into spewing his feelings for you?" Whistling, he set his bowl down and scratched his head. "Wow, that's so random."

"If you met Tony, you'd understand exactly how that happened." She yawned out the words. "You're not the only one with gifts, you know."

"Hrumph." He grunted. "So where does Deidra fit into all this?"

"I'm not entirely sure." She shrugged. "But Tony said he saw a wom-an flying out of the cabin just as he arrived, madder than a swarm of hornets and shrieking obscenities in half English, half Spanish. I can only assume he was talking about Deidra."

"Damn." Erik grimaced in good humor. "I wish I'd been there for that."

"Me too." A smile tugged at Marina's lips, but it died almost im-mediately as she recalled how she'd accused Delaney of lying about his involvement with Deidra. What must he think of her now? The thought made her stomach knot uncomfortably. "Erik?" she asked in despera-tion, "what should I do?"

"Do you love him?"

"Yes." She nodded, biting down on her trembling lip.

"I figured as much." Erik nodded. "If what Tony told you is true, Delaney took a huge risk buying that cabin for you, not knowing whether you'd accept his declaration of love. I guess you need to decide what you're willing to risk for him. And Marina..." His voice took on a cautionary tone. "While I'm pretty damn certain Foster Delaney is nothing like Grayson Munro, *you're* the one who needs to believe it. After everything that's happened over the past few days, though, maybe you should take some time to really think about this."

Marina shook her head. "There *isn't* any time. Tony said Delaney intends to sell the cabin as soon as possible. That's what their appointment was about today."

"Already?" Erik shook his head. "And here I thought Foster was the most levelheaded man I know. I guess that only applies to the boardroom."

"What are you saying?"

"That when it comes to women, Delaney acts as irrationally as any other man in love."

"So you think he bought the cabin because he l-loves me..." She held up a hand on either side of her, balancing them like weights. "But he's selling it for the same reason?"

He took her hands in his. "I think he's tried to treat this whole love thing as a business transaction, because that's what he does best. He *never* loses in the professional arena. But when his logical, business-minded approach to love didn't pan out, he got all flustered and didn't know how to proceed. From what you've told me, it sounds like you've been running a little hot and cold, and that's completely thrown him off his game. He wasn't prepared for it, and since it doesn't fit into his carefully laid out plans, he keeps screwing things up."

Marina chewed at her lip, considering Erik's explanation. She was surprised to find that it actually made a lot of sense. Still, she chafed at the idea of Delaney treating her as a business transaction. "But love is a matter of the heart," she pointed out indignantly.

"And a tricky one at that. Especially in the beginning," he agreed, letting go of her hands to gently squeeze her shoulders. "I have full confidence that you can figure out a way to fix this cluster fudge."

Pulling her from the couch, Erik drew her into his arms for a big bear hug. "But you're in no condition to stress about Delaney tonight." He drew back and pressed a kiss to her forehead. "Get some rest, and clear your head. Tomorrow you'll know what to do—I'm sure of it."

"Is that your gypsy intuition talking?" A teasing smile curved her mouth.

"Let's just call it good advice, shall we?" He tweaked her nose then grabbed his empty bowl, the box of cereal, and the gallon of milk and carried them to the kitchen. Her Majesty trotted along at his heels, meowing loudly in protest, as if she knew he was preparing to leave.

A moment later, Erik reappeared in front of Marina. "See you in the morning." He headed out the door. "Let me know what you decide."

"I will," she promised, watching his retreat down the hall. "Give Jill my love!" she called out.

With a lopsided grin and a lazy salute, Erik disappeared from view.

— —

After wheeling her luggage into the bedroom, Marina clumsily hoisted the bag onto her bed with one hand wrapped around her middle to support her ribs. If she'd been thinking clearly, she would've had Erik do the heavy lifting before he left. But her head had been congested with troubling thoughts since Tony's call, leaving little room for common sense.

With a weary sigh, she turned her attention back to the looming task of unpacking. As she unzipped the suitcase and peeled back the cover, her eyes fell on the sweater that lay on top the pile of garments, and her breath hitched. She lifted it out and burrowed her face in its softness, remembering how Foster had pushed aside its loose neckline to press gentle kisses along her collarbone. The faint scent of Delaney's cologne clung to the garment, and she inhaled it deep into her lungs.

Sinking onto the bed, Marina curled into a fetal position and clutched the sweater to her chest. Soon her mind was drifting in and out of sleep, Erik's words floating through her head.

I'm pretty damn certain Foster Delaney is nothing like Grayson Munro. But you're the one who needs to believe it. You need to decide what you're willing to risk for him.

Marina woke up early on Monday morning, having slept through most of the night. She'd awakened to find Her Majesty's disdainful green-gold gaze watching her from her lofty perch upon the luggage, tail flicking irritably.

"Let me guess," Marina grumbled. "You want something to eat, right?" Shuffling from the bedroom into the kitchen, she filled the cat's food and water bowls and put a pot of coffee on to brew.

"You didn't miss me one bit while I was gone, did you?" The cat didn't bother to look up from her meal, dismissing Marina with an aloof wave of her tail. Marina shrugged, sucked down the last of her coffee, and returned to her room to finish the unpacking she'd left undone the afternoon before.

After emptying the contents of the suitcase, she closed the lid. That's when she noticed the suspicious lump in the outside pocket. Reaching into the compartment, she withdrew a plastic grocery bag containing her mud-caked, doggy-face novelty slippers. She'd completely forgotten about them in the chaos of the weekend's events. But now, memories of everything that had occurred between her and Delaney washed over her, making her heart lurch with regret.

If Foster Delaney had truly loved her before their time in Ogunquit, she couldn't fathom how he could do so now. Not after she'd thrown his confession of love back in his face, along with accusations about his involvement with Deidra.

Reese had been wrong about her. She wasn't the compassionate person he assumed she was. Just as her parents had walked away from their own child, she'd turned her back on Delaney, a man she supposedly loved. She was no better than they were. Worse still, she'd acted as judge and jury, wrongfully convicting Delaney without a fair chance to plead his case. Had she wronged her parents in the same way?

Her eyes flicked over to the nightstand where her cell phone was charging, her resolve wavering. She'd heard somewhere that there are always two sides to every story. While it was true that both Delaney and her parents had made mistakes, Marina herself had yet to consider her own part in those stories. Certainly her abandonment issues had come into play, making her distrustful and slow to excuse others of their faults. Maybe, though, the first step to mending things with her parents, and with Foster Delaney, was to look *inward*...to address the flaws in her own behavior.

As if pleased with Marina's train of thought, Tasha's familiar words floated through her mind. *That's it Mari...let the healing lead you back to Mom and Dad.*

Before she could change her mind, Marina snatched up her cell phone and punched the speed dial for her parents. Three rings later, her mom picked up.

"Marina." Her voice was a relieved sigh. "I wasn't sure you'd call back."

"To tell you the truth, I didn't think I would, either," Marina admitted. "Listen...I'm s-sorry I haven't called since—"

"I know, dear." Her mom sniffled. "Me too. But the important thing is you're calling *now*."

— —

When Marina hung up the phone about ten minutes later, she felt as if an enormous weight had been lifted off her shoulders. A tentative new bond had been forged with her mother, and they'd promised to talk the following week when her father returned from a fishing trip.

An exultant surge of energy and purpose coursed through Marina's veins, fueling her acute need to alleviate the other burden weighing so heavily on her heart. She had to somehow convince Foster Delaney that she was worthy of his love and deserved a second chance.

The problem was, she didn't have a clue how to go about it. Was it foolish of her to think he'd even give her the time of day after she'd treated him so unfairly? What man would do so after risking everything for her? At that despairing thought, Marina shook her head, dropping her face into her hands. "Tasha," she cried out miserably, "what should I do?"

No sooner had the words left her mouth than a memory slipped into her mind. It was the day her sister passed away, and Marina had kept a constant vigil at her bedside. Throughout the day, she'd held Tasha's hand and rubbed her bald head as she faded in and out of consciousness. At one point, Tasha had suddenly become lucid, and they'd talked for nearly fifteen minutes, laughing and crying together as they recalled fond memories.

Falling silent, her sister had stiffened, squeezing Marina's hand with surprising strength. Assuming Tasha was in the throes of her final moments, Marina tried to release her hand to go fetch her parents so they could say their final farewells. But Tasha held fast, giving her head a weak shake.

"Mari," she whispered hoarsely, her breathing growing more labored. "Don't settle for a man...like Grayson," Tasha wheezed. "There is...someone better out there...for you. When you...find him, don't be afraid to...give your whole heart to him," she coughed out.

"Shhh...," Marina admonished as hot tears scalded her eyes. "Don't talk."

"Have to..." The corner of Tasha's mouth curved into a pained smile. "Won't...be here...much longer. Got to...give you...one...last...lecture."

It was hard not to laugh at her sister's morbid sense of humor, so Marina didn't hold back, knowing how it would lift Tasha's spirits.

"'Atta girl," Tasha rasped, her voice a dry, gravely sound. Grimacing, she licked her parched lips. "Risk *everything* for him...f-for your happiness."

They were the last words her sister had uttered.

Marina blinked, swiping away her tears as the memory faded. Just as Erik had told her she would, Marina now knew, with absolute clarity, what she needed to do. Glancing heavenward, she whispered a heartfelt thank you as she sprinted for the shower, anxious to get to work—and Delaney—as quickly as possible.

20

Marina scanned Foster Delaney's office suite in stunned silence.

Though the large mahogany desk, chairs and other pieces of furniture remained, there was no wall art or personal items on the desk to suggest he'd ever worked at Argyle Media Solutions. The realization hit her like a painful blow to the chest, driving the air from her lungs.

He was gone.

It seemed cruel that her decision to resign her position and tell Delaney how she felt had come too late. Or had it? Jumping to conclusions hadn't done her any favors over the past few days. And she couldn't afford to screw one more thing up if there was even the slightest chance to reclaim the man she loved.

She needed more information.

Rushing from Delaney's office suite, she went in search of Suki, relieved to find the woman alone in the small office she shared with one other employee. "Do you have a sec?" Marina asked, wringing her hands.

"Of course," Suki said in a flat tone, her smile hollow.

Marina noted the woman's pensive expression and lackluster eyes. "I'm so sorry about you and Milo." She pushed the door closed behind her.

"Thanks." Suki shrugged dismissively. "But to tell you the truth, Milo hasn't been himself lately."

Marina nodded. "Erik mentioned that."

"Did you know that Deidra Torres has been blackmailing him to get her hands on personal information about Delaney?"

"What?" Marina muttered disbelievingly, sinking into a chair. As she sat there, several memories bubbled to the surface, demanding attention. Milo's suspicious conversation with Deidra at the spring kickoff party. His guilty expression and wariness when she'd caught him watching her at the bank of elevators. Deidra's call to Delaney's private cell phone.

"Yeah." Suki breathed out a shaky sigh. "They've both been fired."

"Oh. I, uh..." Marina struggled for words. As much as she wanted to sympathize with her friend, time was a luxury she just didn't possess at the moment. "Suki, I'd like to talk to you about this later, but there's something I have to ask you. I went to Mr. Delaney's office, but it's been cleared out. Where is he?"

"You didn't hear?" Her almond-shaped eyes widened. "Oh right, I forgot..." She nodded, rubbing her forehead. "Milo mentioned you went away for a few days." Leaning forward, she lowered her voice, even though they were alone in a room. "He quit. His last day was actually last Thursday, but none of us knew about it until today. We just assumed he was on another one of his business trips."

Marina drew her bottom lip between her teeth, kneading it absentmindedly as she tried to recall some of the things Delaney had told her in Ogunquit...

I'm here because you're here. I can't hold my feelings back anymore. I won't. I came out here to tell you that I'm in love with you.

Realization washed over her as the clues floating through her mind coalesced into a solid, definitive truth. Foster Delaney had resigned his position at Argyle Media Solutions *before* he'd arrived at the cabin, a home he'd purchased solely with her in mind. The place where he'd proclaimed his love for her, as a man.

Not as her employer.

Tony had mentioned that Delaney purchased the cabin five or six months ago. And Delaney had told her that he'd loved her since the first day she'd started working as his employee. Surely that depth of devotion could not be discarded so easily over the course of a weekend, regardless of the mistakes and misjudgments that had occurred?

A flicker of hope kindled to life within Marina, and she knew she had to risk everything to find out for sure. Surging to her feet, her words came out in a frantic rush. "Do you know where Delaney is now?"

"No." Suki shook her head. "We haven't seen or heard from him since he quit."

"OK, thanks." Marina handed a folder containing her resignation to Suki. "Give that to whoever's in charge now, will you?" she asked, reaching for the door handle behind her.

"Wait!" her friend called out. "What about your dress?"

"Keep it." Marina smiled as she exited Suki's office. "I'm sure you'll have another opportunity to wear it again real soon." Practically jogging down the hall to her office, she dialed Erik on her cell phone.

"Hey, Rina, what's up?" he answered in his usual I'm-heavily-caffeinated morning voice.

"I need to borrow your car."

"I take it you've made your decision?" Erik said after a meaningful pause. "Are you sure Foster is worth the risk?"

"I'm sure," she confirmed, her voice practically humming with conviction. "Please hurry."

She smiled when Erik suddenly started shouting obscenities at other drivers over the din of the Maxima's revving engine and the blaring of car horns in the background. "I'll be there in ten!" he promised.

"I'll be waiting outside the building." Marina quickly collected her personal belongings and headed for the bank of elevators.

There was only one place she could think to search for her former employer. She just hoped that her instinct was correct and she'd still find him there. But more than that, she prayed that he would be willing to accept her apology.

And her love.

— ~

About thirty-eight minutes later, Marina pulled up in front of the cabin in Ogunquit. All was still except for the soft whisper of leaves rustling in the October breeze.

There were no cars in the gravel drive, no one milling about outside. A realtor's blue and white "For Sale" sign was the only glaring blemish on the otherwise placid scene. It bothered her to think Delaney was in such a hurry to discard all memory of her, and she felt a mad urge to rip the sign out of the ground and toss it into a nearby cluster of birch trees. As she traversed the driveway and stepped onto the porch, she tried to tamp down the fear that she was too late.

Hesitating at the window near the front door, Marina held a hand to the glass and peeked into the cabin's interior. It was spotless and tidy, giving little indication that two people had temporarily resided here as recently as yesterday. *You might as well leave now...no one's here,* the voice of doubt murmured through her.

Heaving a sigh, she was about to turn away when, on impulse, she reached out and curled her hand over the door's ornate handle. Her heart raced as she gave the lever a tentative little push.

The door swung open.

"Hello?" Marina called out as she stepped into the foyer.

There was no answer.

Her gaze swept over the great room and up the stairs. Moving over to the dining area, she craned her neck and peered into the kitchen. "Hello?" Once again, her greeting was met with a deafening silence.

Delaney was well and truly gone.

Her attempt at making a grand romantic gesture, as Tony would call it, had failed. The shock of defeat held her immobile, despair covering her like a blanket. Adding to her misery, the room was emotionally charged with memories. Her gaze slid to the bare dining table where the cheerful arrangement of ivory roses and white daisies had welcomed her for a late breakfast on Saturday. She lifted her eyes to the kitchen cabinet where Delaney had hemmed her in, his closeness making her pulse skitter erratically and his husky voice sending a jolt of longing through her. *I'm. Here. For. You.*

Delaney's words played through her mind like a mocking chorus, a cruel reminder that he was gone for good, that he'd never be here again. Feeling a wretchedness of mind and spirit as acute as any physical pain, Marina stumbled into the great room and collapsed upon the sofa. Dropping her face into her hands, she gave in to her despair and let the tears flow.

"Marina?"

She heard the echo of Delaney's voice in her head and knew it was time to go home and leave the cabin and its memories behind. Now that she was unemployed, she was free to go wherever she wished to escape the places and things that reminded her of him.

But even as she thought it, she knew she couldn't leave Erik and Jill, or the little one they were expecting. Moving away was out of the question right now, but a new job free from any association with Delaney would offer a much-needed distraction, she decided.

"Marina?"

There was his voice again, louder, and more insistent. It seemed so real that her nerves tingled with awareness, and she couldn't resist the temptation to turn toward the sound.

Foster Delaney stood in the foyer.

"*Foster,*" she breathed out his name as she came to her feet. Her eyes drank in the sight of him, from his relaxed-fit jeans and gray blazer, to the untucked white and lavender striped shirt he wore, slightly rumpled and unbuttoned at the neck. His eyes looked puffy, and his dark hair was ungroomed, short tufts sticking out every which way. The man looked as though he hadn't slept for days, but to Marina, he was the most beautiful sight she'd ever seen.

"What are you doing here?" he inquired in a dull voice, his expression tight.

"I called out, but no one answered," she replied lamely, deliberately ignoring his question. She would not allow the hurt and doubt kindled by his stinging indifference to deter her from her goal of telling him how she felt once and for all.

Delaney shoved his hands in his jeans pockets. "Reese got us all the way out to the interstate before I realized I hadn't locked the door." He grimaced.

"Oh." Knowing just how close she'd come to missing him tied her stomach in knots. She gave in to the familiarity of her anxious quirk and began to gnaw at her bottom lip, casting about for something to say. "How's your ankle?" she blurted out.

"The swelling's gone down a little, but it's still tender." He shrugged. "Your ribs?"

"About the same." Marina wound a hand around her middle, but the gesture had more to do with calming her stomach than the state of her healing injury. "I, uh...never thanked you properly for taking care of me after my accident—"

A shadow of annoyance crossed his face. "Is that why you came back?" he retorted, his eyes hardening. "To thank me?"

"No. Yes. Both. I mean—" Marina broke off midsentence, shaking her head in frustration. It was impossible to think straight under the steady scrutiny of Delaney's flinty green gaze. Drawing in a calming breath, she tried again. "I spoke with Suki this morning. She told me you resigned your position at Argyle. Is that true?"

"It is." He shrugged noncommittally. "But it hardly matters anymore."

"It matters to me." Marina tilted her chin up.

"Does it?" The bitterness in his voice lashed out at her. "Yesterday you were so convinced I was fooling around with Deidra Torres that you couldn't get away from me fast enough."

"I know." Her cheeks burned with humiliation. "I'm sorry. It was wrong of me to make that assumption."

"While I appreciate that," Delaney responded flatly, glancing behind him, "I've kept Reese waiting too long. So if you don't mind..." He swept a hand toward the open door.

Marina's resolve faltered. There was nothing in the unyielding set of his features, the grim line of his mouth, or his blank, fixed eyes to support the hope that had flared to life earlier and compelled her to chase after the intractable man standing before her now. All she saw was an expression of pained tolerance.

Delaney cleared his throat with an impatient grunt, motioning pointedly at the door.

Determined to show him how unaffected she was by his rejection, Marina kept her face and voice carefully neutral. "I'm sorry to have inconvenienced you." Squaring her shoulders, she tucked a stray lock of hair behind her ear and forced her legs into motion. All she had to do was make it to the car, and then she could cry all the way back to Portland if she felt like it. But she refused to shed a tear in front of Foster Delaney. Pressing her lips into a firm line, she focused her gaze on the open door ahead and swept past the man she knew would haunt her for the rest of her days.

Just as Marina was about to slip out the cabin door, Tasha's last words rang in her ears as vividly as if her sister had been standing right beside her.

Risk everything for the man you love...for your happiness!

With her heart in her throat, Marina took a step back and pushed the door closed. Spinning around, she nearly crashed into Delaney, who was so close she could feel the heat radiating from his lean frame. His eyes registered surprise, conflicting emotions following one another in quick succession across his face, before a look of withdrawal slipped over his expression. Stepping away from her, he crossed his arms over his chest. "Marina, what are you—"

Her hand flew up to halt his protest. "I can't leave without telling you how I feel."

Delaney stiffened. "I think I heard enough about how you feel yesterday," he muttered.

"It was wrong of me to treat you as I did." Marina nodded. "I should have trusted you, or at least let you explain." She drew in a quick breath and plunged forward. "I know I have no right to ask you to believe me after everything that's happened, but I do love you. In fact, I've loved you for a long time."

Desperately searching his face for a reaction and finding no access to his unreadable features, she swallowed her disappointment, lifted her chin, and boldly met his eyes. "I just wanted you to know that."

Still no reaction.

Delaney didn't so much as press his lips into a hard line or exhibit a tightening of the jaw. He just stared at her with a stony-eyed gaze.

After a long pause, she nodded in understanding. So that was it, then.

Willing her legs to move, Marina turned her back on him. This time she would walk away for good. She'd risked everything—her job, her pride, and her heart. But at least she'd never have to live with the regret of not fighting for the one thing she wanted most in this life.

21

Marina yanked the front door open, desperate to escape the cabin and its owner.

Before she could step over the threshold, a hand shot out and yanked her back inside. The door slammed shut behind her as she was spun around and crushed against the hard wall of Foster Delaney's chest.

"Marina, what took you so damn long?" he choked out, burying his face in her hair. "I've been dying inside since you left."

A cry of relief broke from her lips as she slipped her arms around his neck and leaned into him. "I'm so sorry," she whispered against his throat, her tears wetting the collar of his shirt. "Please forgive me."

He pulled back and framed her face with his hands, the pads of his thumbs gently swiping at her damp cheeks. "If you'll forgive me for being such an ass." He stared into her eyes, letting her see all the tenderness that shone in their depths. "I never meant for things to get so out of hand." He grimaced. "In my own screwy way, I was only trying to show you how much I—"

"Delaney?" She stopped him with a finger to his lips. "Stop talking, and just kiss me already."

Foster chuckled. "Have I told you how much I love it when you boss me around?" A grin overtook his handsome features, revealing the twin divots in his cheeks.

Marina melted inside. She hadn't realized how much she'd missed those dimples! Over the past few days, there'd been so few reasons for either of them to smile. But that had all changed now. She made a silent vow to make Foster smile like this every day for the rest of their lives so his dimples would be on permanent display for her viewing pleasure.

"Not as much as I love these." Tilting her face up, she pressed a kiss to each dimple. "But Delaney, there's too much talking going on."

"Marina," he chastised, taking her hands and pulling her further into the room. "I haven't been your employer since last Thursday." Catching her chin between his thumb and forefinger, he lifted her face to meet his gaze. "If you want me to kiss you, I insist that you call me Foster."

"Fine." She dragged him to a stop. "Kiss me *now*, Foster."

His mouth was on hers so fast there was no time to catch her breath. But breathing was the last thing on her mind. All Marina could think about was the man kissing her lips and how she wanted him to kiss her like this forever.

"Mr. Delaney?"

They broke apart at the sound of Reese's startled voice. The chauffeur stood just inside the door, gawking at them.

"Miss Marina!" he exclaimed, a smile spreading over his whole face. "I was wondering whose car that was out front. Then, when Mr. Delaney didn't come out after a while, why, I started to fret."

"Not to worry, Reese." Marina moved back into Foster's embrace, her smile eager and affectionate as he pulled her tight against him and placed a kiss on the crown of her head. "He's in good hands."

"Oh, I know he is, Miss Marina." Reese chuckled. "I know he is."

"Why don't you take the rest of the day off," Foster suggested to Reese, his eyes never leaving hers. "Go spend some time with your wife. I'll call you later."

"Yes, Mr. Delaney. I'll do that. Thank you, sir."

But Marina was pretty sure Foster never heard the chauffeur's response, because his attention was fully engaged elsewhere.

On her lips.

— ~

"I still can't believe you came back." Foster rested his cheek against the top of Marina's head.

They had spent the afternoon kissing and touching each other, as if it would take years to make up for the short period of time they'd been separated. Now they snuggled on the sofa, Foster's arms wrapped around her in a possessive embrace, a cheerful fire crackling in the hearth before them.

"I almost didn't." Marina pulled out of Foster's arms, eliciting a grunt of protest. She considered kissing away his objection but knew it would lead to other activities best left until after they'd said what needed to be said. "When I left here yesterday morning, there was little reason to believe I should."

"What made you change your mind?" he prompted, brushing a lock of her hair behind her ear. He continued to touch her as if he feared that she might disappear if he didn't maintain constant contact with her body.

"Well, first, Tony called and told me why you'd purchased the cabin, and that—"

"Wait, what?" Foster held up a hand. "Tony Carmichael, the real estate guy from Ogunquit, called *you*?"

"Mmm hmm." She nodded, unable to resist the smile curving her lips in response to his adorably puzzled expression.

"How do you even know him?"

Marina gave him a teasing nudge. "I have spies in every corner of Maine, you know."

"Is that so?" He cocked an amused brow. "Well, it's good to know there's at least one person in *my* little corner of the world who's willing to go to bat for me."

"Actually, there are more than you know." She smoothed the lines of astonishment creasing his forehead. "I'd convinced myself that I'd lost you. But the memory of something Tasha said the day she died changed my mind about coming after you."

Foster grabbed her hand again, interlacing his fingers with hers. "What did she say?" he prompted softly.

Marina met his eyes with a tender gaze. "That there was someone better for me than Grayson, and when I found him, I shouldn't be afraid to surrender my whole heart to him. She told me to risk *everything* for the man—and the life—I want."

"I'm so grateful you listened." He grazed her cheek with the knuckles of his free hand.

"Me too." Marina leaned into his caress. "Believe it or not, something Erik said actually had a lot to do with me being here as well. Plus, he loaned me his car so I could hunt you down."

"Remind me to thank him." Foster sounded relieved. "Yesterday morning, I was a little worried he'd make good on your threat to run over my foot!"

"He might do worse than that if you hurt me," she said with a wry smile. "He's extremely protective. But he's also very fair and sensible. It was Erik who actually questioned your involvement with Deidra."

Foster threw up his hands. "I can't believe *anyone* would think I'd get involved with that woman!"

"I know." She flushed with guilt. "But you have to admit it looked pretty bad when Deidra showed up *here*, especially after her call the night before." She bit down on her lip to stop herself from asking him why Deidra had turned up at the cabin. After treating Foster so unfairly, she was loath to give him the slightest impression that she might still mistrust him.

"I suppose it did," he conceded, rubbing the back of his neck. "Believe me, after I fired her Thursday, on my last day as CEO at Argyle, she was the last person I expected—or wanted—to see *here*." His eyes searched hers, silently pleading with her to believe him before he went on. He must have found the answer he was looking for, because he continued without further prompting.

"After you left yesterday, I threatened to have Deidra carted off to Maine Correctional Center if she didn't provide me with details of how and why she was filching my personal information. Turns out, Deidra's a chronic blackmailer. That's how she's always gotten what she wants out of life—money, perks, sex, whatever. Anyway, she produced a photocopy of that paper I showed you Wednesday, the one with the cabin's information on it, which she got from Milo, along with my private cell phone number. When I pushed her for more information she started sobbing uncontrollably—I don't know if she was acting, or actually scared that I'd have her incarcerated—but it was hard to make out what she was saying. I'm pretty sure she said something about seduction and bribery, though. Fortunately, it didn't come to that. Milo, on the other hand, didn't escape so easily."

Marina shook her head. "Kind of makes you wonder who else Deidra was blackmailing at Argyle."

"Probably more than we care to know about." He grimaced. "That woman collects secrets like people collect pins on Pinterest. Apparently, Milo was guilty of some recent misconduct that would have resulted in his termination from Argyle. Deidra sniffed out the details and threatened to spill the beans if he didn't do exactly as she said. He was afraid of losing his job, and Suki, so he went along with Deidra's little scheme. It's sad, you know? I think Milo really cared about Suki." Foster fell silent, his expression pensive.

Marina sat quietly beside him, holding his hand while she let him indulge his thoughts. Finally, he blew out a shaky breath. "I came so close to losing _you_."

She laid her hand against his cheek. "Well, I'm here now. And you're _not_ going to lose me, no matter how hard you try."

"In that case," his voice caught on a strained half laugh, "I should probably warn you that I don't plan on trying very hard."

"I can live with that."

In one swift motion, Foster gathered her against his chest and brought her down on top of him as he fell back onto the sofa cushions. His hands skimmed a seductive path down the sides of her breasts, trailing over the curves of her waist and hips to cup her bottom and press her body against his.

Marina's stomach grumbled loudly.

Foster raised his brows in a teasing expression. "I'm pretty sure I've never had that particular effect on a woman before."

"I'm sorry." Her face flushed with embarrassment. "I haven't eaten since this morning."

"Why didn't you say something?" Foster brought them to a sitting position.

She nibbled at her lip. "Uh, I was a little busy trying to win you back. And then you kind of distracted me with kisses and, well...other things."

"I did, didn't I?" He smiled mischievously. "Just a head's up...I'm about ready to distract you again."

As Foster leaned in to nuzzle her neck, Marina shot off the couch. "Oh no you don't!" Laughing, she rounded the sofa and headed for the kitchen. But she didn't get far.

"Wait!" His hand shot out and clamped around her wrist. Hauling her back around to face him, Foster dropped to his knees. "Marry me, Marina. Tomorrow, or the next day. Or the day after that. Just say you'll be my wife by the end of the week."

Her heart flipped over at his proposal. But everything was happening so fast, and after the emotional turmoil of the past few days, she needed some time to process it all. Grayson had rushed their relationship, and look how that had turned out. She wanted something different with Foster. She wanted to savor every aspect of their courtship as it progressed naturally toward marriage, to relish each phase of the wedding planning process; to experience the building anticipation as their special day drew close.

She envisioned a small evening ceremony, surrounded by their closest friends and family members. A canopy of fairy lights would twinkle overhead, and bouquets of white daisies and ivory roses would decorate every table, cover every surface, their fragrance filling the air as she and Foster repeated their vows.

But in the midst of fantasizing about a longer courtship and planning the perfect wedding, Marina had an epiphany.

She realized that while she and Foster had never dated in the physical sense, their hearts had been courting one another since the day they'd met. And then there was the fact that since that night at the pub—was it only ten days ago?—their relationship had already endured, and survived, more turbulence and growing pains than it might have done if they'd experienced a much longer courtship.

The revelation hit her with the force of a tsunami wave. In that moment, Marina knew she wanted to marry Foster Delaney as soon as possible, to belong to him in a way that only a wife could. She simply needed more than a few days to plan the ceremony she felt they deserved. Since she was unemployed now, she could spend all day, every day, making arrangements. And with Tony's help, Marina believed she'd be able to pull off a memorable wedding in just under a month. Tony would be so excited when she gave him the news!

She heard Foster curse and immediately snapped back to awareness.

"No matter what I do, or how hard I try, you're never going to let this work, are you?" Dropping her hands, he stood abruptly and stalked toward the door.

Marina could only watch in stunned disbelief as Foster disappeared into the dark October night. Her confusion soon gave way to a stark realization.

Foster had mistaken her silence as another rejection.

22

Marina was sick with worry.

Nearly two hours had passed since Foster had walked out on her. After the first thirty minutes, she'd gone outside to look for him, thinking he'd simply stepped outside for some air. When her search of both the front and back yards had yielded no results, she'd skirted the surrounding perimeter of the forest, calling out his name. But the only responses were the chirping of insects and the rustling of leaves in the night breeze. Disheartened, she'd returned to the cabin, where she now paced back and forth between the dining area, foyer, and great room.

After the initial shock of Foster's departure, she'd grown angry with him for taking off without giving her a chance to explain herself. But her indignation had quickly dissipated when she remembered how she'd done the same thing to him only a few days before.

Concern had quickly replaced her anger as she thought of Foster wandering around in the dark on his sprained ankle. What if he got attacked by a wild animal? What if he'd done further damage to his injured ankle and was lying hurt somewhere out in the forest? Her stomach clenched at the thought. She'd never be able to forgive herself if he came to any harm because she hesitated at his proposal.

She could take Erik's car and search the main roads, but something told her she wouldn't find Foster there, and she wasn't about to traipse through an unfamiliar forest at night, alone. Gnawing at her thumbnail, Marina began to wonder if she shouldn't start calling the local authorities and area hospitals. Almost immediately, she decided against it and dialed Reese's number instead. She felt guilty for calling when Foster had given him the rest of the day off, but she was desperate at this point. Her anxiety only heightened when he didn't pick up.

With trembling fingers, Marina punched in the cell phone number for the only other person she could think to call.

"Marina!" Tony picked up on the second ring. "What exciting news do you have for me?"

She'd promised to keep him informed of any developments with Foster, but this wasn't exactly the news she'd hoped to deliver. "I need your help." The words spilled out of her mouth in a frantic rush. "Foster's run off, and his ankle is sprained, and it's dark, and he doesn't have a coat, and he's been gone for two hours and—"

Surprisingly, Tony had no trouble making sense of her rambling. "Don't you worry about a thing, sweetie," he answered in a motherly tone that instantly soothed her. "Jake and I will be there as soon as we can. We'll bring Lucas and Hawk, too. Between the five of us, I'm sure we'll find him."

"Um, I'm not entirely sure Lucas will want to come." In fact, she wouldn't doubt it if Lucas were content to let Foster stay lost.

But twenty minutes later, he stood in the cabin's foyer, along with Tony and Jake, deliberating over their search and rescue plans. Hawk paced about them anxiously, as if sensing the forthcoming hunt. Marina wasn't sure that was such a good thing. The last time Hawk was in the same room with Foster, his snarl had hinted at a fierce desire to tear the man's limbs off.

With that grim thought, she hastily turned her attention back to the group. "We can take Delaney's golf cart," she offered when Tony brought up the logistics of transportation. "It has headlights and space for four people. It will be faster than walking."

Lucas shook his head. "You three take the golf cart," he suggested. "Hawk and I will go on foot. He's actually a half-decent tracker. Marina, you got anythin' that'll help him pick up Foster's scent?"

Marina's gaze shifted to the gray blazer haphazardly draped over the back of the couch. She'd helped Foster shrug out of it earlier in the day, when their kissing had turned into more amorous activities. Her face flushed with heat, and she was pretty sure Tony knew exactly what she was thinking, because he flashed her a knowing smile as she handed the jacket over to Lucas.

"Any ideas where we should start looking first?" Jake asked the group.

His words made something click in Marina's head. "Foster took me to some kind of druid grove near here. Let's start there."

— ⁓

"He's not here."

It was like a déjà vu of Foster's empty office all over again. Disappointment sat like a heavy stone in Marina's stomach as she circled the deserted grove, the beam of her flashlight bobbing as her boots crunched across the frozen unevenness of the forest floor. "Foster brought me here on Saturday," she murmured. "He said he spent a lot of time here after his wife died. I was almost certain this is where he'd come."

Jake gave her shoulder a reassuring squeeze. "Don't worry, Marina. We'll find him."

She tried to muster a convincing smile, wondering how Lucas's search was going. He and Hawk had taken the path at the back of the cabin, with a plan to search the forest as they approached the druid grove from the opposite direction.

"I don't think this is a druid grove," Tony informed them as they met at the center of the clearing. "I watched a show on ancient Native American mound builders, and this"—he swept his LED lantern over the embankment surrounding a circular area of flat earth—"definitely resembles the structure and style of the earthen mounds they used to construct."

Jake rolled his eyes indulgently. "We can discuss its origin later. Will you please focus?" He shook his head and turned back to Marina with an apologetic expression. "I really need to wean him off the idiot box," he whispered. "Lately, he's developed an annoying habit of referencing pretty much everything to a television program."

"I heard that!" Tony fisted his hands on his hips. "For your information, that idiot box has saved your derriere on more than one occasion. Where do you think I learned to hem your pants and cook your fancy French dinners?" Giving Jake a pointed look, he sidled past him to hug Marina to his side.

"How are you holding up, sweetie?"

"Oh, Tony." She let her head sag against his shoulder. "This is all my fault! If I hadn't hesitated when Foster proposed—"

"He *proposed*?" Tony reiterated in an exaggerated tone, his voice humming with barely contained excitement.

"Mmm hmm," she sniffled, her breath frosting in the frigid night air. "H-he wanted to get married by the end of the week—"

"Whoa, that's fast," Jake interjected.

Marina nodded. "It completely caught me off guard. I mean, so much has happened between us in such a short time. It took me a few minutes to process everything, you know? Unfortunately, by the time I finally realized that I *do* want to marry Foster, just as soon as we can make reasonable arrangements, I'd waited too long to answer him, and he—"

"Took that as a no," Jake finished for her, his voice sympathetic.

Marina closed her eyes, shuddering as she recalled the moment in vivid detail.

"Well, what are we all standing around for?" Tony released Marina and brought his hands together in two short staccato claps. "We have a fiancé to find, people!"

"Um, Tony, I'm *not* engaged," she reminded him in a trembling voice.

"Not *yet!*" he quipped, emphasizing his point with a lofty shimmy of his head. "But we're going to hunt your runaway groom down and set him straight before he screws me out of a perfectly good opportunity to help you plan a wedding!"

Marina choked out a half laugh, her mood lightening at his words.

"Now, if Lucas would just hurry up..." Tony's head swished back and forth, his gaze sweeping the fringe of trees lining the grove.

As if on cue, Lucas and Hawk crashed through the trees from somewhere behind them, eliciting a startled squeal from Tony. "There you are!" He blew out a relieved breath. "Any luck?"

"I'm pretty sure we're onto Foster's scent, but..." Lucas hesitated, scrubbing a hand over his face.

A disquieting feeling shivered through Marina when she saw the look of concern creasing his features. "W-what is it?"

Fisting his hands on his hips, Lucas released an audible swoosh of air through his teeth. "If the trail *is* his, there's a possibility he's injured. We, uh... found a trail of blood, too."

Marina gasped, unaware that she was swaying until Tony and Jake reached out to steady her.

Lucas gave her an apologetic grimace but wasted no time attempting to soften the blow with reassuring words. Instead, he hastily whispered something to Tony and disappeared again through the trees.

"Let's go, hon. Lucas can take it from here." Tony steered her toward the golf cart. When she hesitated, glancing over her shoulder in the direction Lucas had gone, she heard Tasha's voice in her head. *Go with your friends, Mari...everything will work out.*

Tony placed his hand in the small of her back and gave her a gentle nudge. "Lucas said he'd meet us back at the cabin as soon as he locates Foster."

But this time, neither Tony's words of reassurance nor the comforting voice of her beloved sister could silence Marina's fears.

— ~

Marina clutched a warm mug in her hands, methodically rubbing the smooth, ceramic surface with her thumb.

It felt as though hours and hours had passed since she, Tony, and Jake had returned from the druid grove. In reality, it had been just over an hour or so. But each minute that ticked by without word of Foster threatened to drive her mad.

"Would you like another cup of chamomile tea?" Tony's voice managed to crack through Marina's gloomy thoughts.

She gave him a weak shake of her head, staring blankly at the mug in front of her. She'd already had enough of the warm beverage to keep her peeing every five minutes or so for the rest of the night. And thus far, it had done little to calm her nerves. Vaguely, she was aware of Jake getting up from the table and moving about, but her mind continued to drift. The sudden clinking of glasses in front of her finally snapped Marina's attention back to the present moment.

"I think you could use something a little stronger than tea right now." Jake poured three snifters of wine and handed one to Marina. "Besides," he said, apparently sensing her reluctance, "you need to help us toast our anniversary."

Marina's head snapped up. "It's your anniversary?" Her startled gaze flicked between the two men. "Why didn't you say something before?"

"Didn't seem right"—Jake shrugged—"under the present circumstances."

"That's just great." She dropped her face into her hands, shaking her head. "I managed to ruin Foster's proposal *and* your anniversary in one night!"

"You didn't ruin anything." Jake waved off her distress. "Tony did that the minute he tuned into reality TV."

"Oh nonsense," Tony huffed. "We'd already moved beyond the highlight of the evening."

Marina tilted her head, considering them with raised brows.

"Jake surprised me with plane tickets to Paris!"

"How wonderful." Marina smiled genuinely, trying to soak up the excitement radiating off of Tony. Heaven knew she could use all the mood boosting she could get at this point, and she was grateful for the distraction. "That's definitely toast worthy," she said, raising her glass in the air.

Following her lead, Tony and Jake lifted their snifters to hers in a jaunty clink that ended abruptly as the cabin's front door flew open.

"*Foster!*" Marina's glass tumbled from her hand, but she hardly cared about the violet liquid dribbling into her lap. Needing to know that he wasn't a figment of her imagination, she catapulted across the room and flung herself into his arms.

"*Oof!*" He stumbled back from the force of the impact, almost toppling into Lucas. Steadying himself, Foster swept her against him with one arm, burrowing his face into her hair. "Marina," he mumbled against her neck.

"Don't ever do that to me again." She thumped his chest with her fist. "I was so worried about you."

"I'm sorry I ran out like that." Foster flattened her fist against his chest, his hand curling around hers. "It really threw me when you didn't respond to my proposal. I thought..." He shook his head. "I couldn't think properly, only feel. And what I felt—" He broke off, swallowing hard. "I needed to cool off before I said—or did—anything stupid."

"Well, you *did* do something stupid." Marina pulled her hand from his, shaking her head in disbelief. "I can't believe you were gone for over two hours in freezing temperatures, without a coat. Plus, you were alone out in the dark, with a sprained ankle!"

"Actually, it took less than ten minutes for me to cool off," he admitted sheepishly. "The rest of the time I was just, well...lost."

"And bleeding," Lucas supplied in a glib tone.

Foster shot him an irritated glance.

It was then that Marina noticed Foster's other arm hanging limply at his side beneath the gray blazer draped over his shoulders. Carefully nudging the jacket aside, she saw a jagged hole in his left shirt sleeve, revealing a blood-tinged bandage underneath.

She delicately fingered the bandage, her anxious gaze lifting to Foster's. "H-how bad is it?"

"Despite the fact that your friend here had me stitched up by a vet, I think I'll live."

"A vet?" Marina arched a brow at Lucas, who merely shrugged.

"He was the only doctor available at the time."

Marina shook her head. It seemed Lucas hadn't quite had his fill of pushing Foster's buttons. Well, now wasn't the time. She had other things she was anxious to discuss with Foster. Preferably, without an audience.

To her relief, Tony suddenly blurted out, "We really have to ske-daddle, honey." His eyes glittered with a knowing look, as if he'd just read her mind, and Marina offered him a grateful smile.

Jake retrieved their coats and escorted Tony to the door, tossing a look back at Lucas. "You coming?"

"Nah, Hawk's still keyed up over our adventure tonight. I'm gonna let him walk it off."

"Where is Hawk?" Marina asked.

"I left him out back." Lucas held Foster's gaze, his brown eyes sparking with challenge. "Who knows, he could be turning the hot tub into a doggy bath as we speak."

She felt Foster briefly stiffen next to her. But he merely shrugged, his voice resigned. "I suppose he's earned it after tonight."

The two men seemed to have reached some sort of understanding in that moment, because they exchanged a quick nod of acknowledgment.

Marina walked Lucas through the dining room to the sliding-glass doors where, sure enough, they saw Hawk happily bobbing in the hot tub. They shared a laugh, which quickly turned into an awkward silence. Lucas cleared his throat. "So...you and bonehead, huh?"

"Yep. Thanks to you and Hawk, I'll be Mrs. Bonehead very soon."

Lucas's solemn gaze searched hers for a moment before he spoke. "You sure about this?"

"More sure than I've been about anything else in my entire life." As she said the words aloud, Marina felt the truth of them rippling through her in little waves of pure joy, and something else. Peace.

"Well, if that changes, you know where to find me." With a conspiratorial wink, Lucas slipped out the door.

Finally alone, Marina settled next to Foster on the sofa.

"Why didn't you go to the druid grove?" she asked him. "We looked for you there first."

"That's where I was headed. But it was so stinking dark out there, and I think I mistook a naturally scarred trunk for one of the man-made markings in the trees. By the time I realized I'd veered off the path, I was already lost."

"And this?" She gently ran her fingers over his bandaged arm. "How did it happen?"

"As near as I could tell, a splintered tree branch, laced with a razor-sharp coating of ice, is responsible for that nasty little gash. Shortly after it happened, I heard the howl of what sounded like a wolf and figured it was tracking the scent of my blood. I thought I was a dead man, especially when I saw two glowing eyes and a huge dark shadow crashing through the trees. Fortunately, it turned out to be Hawk." Foster gave his head a rueful shake. "In that moment, all I could think about was never seeing your face again."

Marina's eyes blurred with tears. She knew *exactly* what that felt like. She'd experienced the same bleakness when she'd almost stumbled from the cliff's edge on Marginal Way, and again this morning, when she feared Foster was lost to her forever.

"As a businessman, it was always my job to close multi-million-dollar deals, and I was damn good at it, too." With whisper-soft strokes, Foster used the pad of his thumb to swipe away the tears sliding down her cheeks. "But when you didn't agree to marry me—" He broke off mid-sentence, his voice thick with emotion. "I felt like I'd failed to close the most important deal of my life."

"I never said I *wouldn't* marry you," Marina interjected. "It's just that, well, it's been a rough year, and the past week has been particularly *overwhelming*. Then suddenly, everything was happening so fast, and I-I just needed some time to process it all."

"I know that now, and I feel terrible about running off the minute things looked like they weren't going *my* way. It was selfish of me. I should've stayed and—"

Marina stopped him with a finger to his lips. "The way I see it, we're even. If you'll recall, I basically did the same thing when I ran away from you on Saturday." Framing his face with her hands, she leaned her forehead against his. "Just promise me that you'll never let us run away from each other again."

Foster pulled his face from her grasp, chuckling at Marina's murmured protest. Leaning forward, he pressed his lips to her ear. "That's a promise I intend to keep from now on."

Epilogue

Everyone cheered when Suki caught Marina's bouquet.

But no one whooped louder than Lucas Reynolds. The man hadn't been able to keep his eyes off the petite Asian woman since Marina had introduced them before the ceremony. Suki looked stunning in the teal dress Marina had given her, with her glossy black hair in a loose side bun and the telltale glow of love at first sight haloing her alabaster skin.

Marina beamed at the happy couple as Tony appeared next to her with a playful bump to the shoulder. "Thinking of the upcoming wedding night delights, are we?"

She ignored his comment and directed his attention to Lucas and Suki, heads together as they giggled like a pair of high school kids. "I think I just found your next set of clients."

Tony crossed his arms and pursed his lips as he appraised the couple in question. Within seconds, a mischievous gleam twinkled in his brown eyes, and a saucy little smile tugged at his lips. "Those two will be lucky if they make it through the day without christening Lucas's floor, sofa, *and* bed."

"Tony!" Marina slapped his arm, but her grin matched his own.

"No offense, sweetie, but please don't help me find any more clients. At this rate, Jake and I will never make it to Paris in April. I've already got two weddings lined up, including Erik's, and I haven't even hung out the official wedding planner shingle yet."

Despite his attempts at pouting, Marina knew he was tickled pink. The idea to segue his career into wedding planning had originally taken root when he'd offered to investigate venues for Erik's nuptials. But after successfully pulling together a marriage ceremony and reception as stunning as Marina's—in fourteen days— word had quickly spread. Several people had even approached Tony after the ceremony, and she'd heard guests raving about Jake's delectable refreshments.

"Well, you have nothing but your own talent to blame." Marina swept her arm out to indicate the sea-themed splendor that surrounded them. Under Tony's ministrations, the interior of Foster's cabin had been transformed into a coastal paradise bedecked in aqua, sand, and ivory accents, with bouquets of white chrysanthemums, daisies, and ivory roses. White lanterns topped tables of sea blue, and iridescent aqua fabric strung with twinkly fairy lights created a glowing canopy overhead. She couldn't have asked for a more perfect setting for her wedding.

"She's right, you know." Erik sidled up to Tony, giving him a congratulatory slap on the back. "If our wedding—he bobbed his head at Jill—"is anything like this, you're going to be inundated with more business than you can handle."

Tony's chest swelled with pride and Marina wondered if the buttons on his snug black silk shirt were in danger of popping off. The thought made her grin, but her smile quickly slipped when she noticed the way Jill sagged against Erik's side. "Feeling queasy again?"

Jill nodded. "I'm so ticked off. I really wanted to gorge myself on Jake's divine food, but..." She held a hand over her mouth and swallowed.

"You poor dove." Tony slipped his arm through Jill's. "You come with me, sweetie. We'll get you some ginger ale for your tummy, and then I'll get you settled in your car while Erik says good-bye to Marina." Tony held out his hand for Erik's keys and led a grateful Jill toward the kitchen.

Erik stared after the receding pair with a bemused expression on his face. "Can I hire him as a nanny?"

"He's amazing, isn't he?" Marina laughed. "But you won't need him. You and Jill are going to make incredible parents."

"I know Jill can handle the baby. I was actually thinking of hiring Tony as my own personal nanny."

She rolled her eyes and shoved him in the direction of the kitchen. "Go take care of Jill, already."

But he swiveled around and pulled her into a big bear hug. "I'm so happy for you, Rina." He kissed her forehead. "And I'm glad Foster turned out to be the guy I suspected he was. I guess my gypsy intuition doesn't totally suck after all."

"No. No, it doesn't." Marina sighed happily. "He's everything you said he was. And so much more."

"Well, Mr. So-Much-More is headed this way, so I'd better surrender you to your groom and get back to my own ailing bride to be." Releasing her with a little shove in Foster's direction, he backed toward the kitchen. "You did good, by the way...inviting your parents to the wedding."

Marina nodded in acknowledgment, thinking how Tasha must have thought so, too. Shortly after her parents had arrived, the feather light imprint of an embrace fluttered over her skin, and Marina felt her beloved sister's presence withdraw. To her surprise, it hadn't saddened her the way she thought it might. In fact, for the first time since Tasha's death, she felt completely at peace. And with that realization came another. Her nervous lip biting now seemed a thing of the past.

"Talk to you soon, Erik." Marina waved in farewell, just as her husband's strong arms slid around her waist and pulled her against his firm chest.

"I have a surprise for you." Foster's husky voice whispered against her ear. "Are you ready to get out of here?"

"Mmm hmm." She drew in a shaky breath as visions of the wedding night delights Tony had mentioned sent a shiver of anticipation through her body.

Taking her by the hand, Foster pulled her toward the door, his eyes glittering with expectation as he swung it open. Marina could hardly believe what she was seeing. Just beyond the front porch stood a white, horse-drawn wagon, the back filled with a bed of hay and heaped with blue-and-white fleece blankets and pillows.

"Lucas actually gave me the idea." There was a nervous edge to Foster's voice, as if he feared he'd been fed a bad piece of advice. "He said there was something about the way you looked at one of his book covers."

"Autumn in Your Arms," she murmured. "It was an image of a couple laying together in the back of a hay wagon, and I remember wishing that couple could be us."

"And now it can be." Foster brushed his knuckles along her cheek. Silently, he drew her over to the wagon and helped her up, nimbly leaping in after her. Once they were settled under the warm pile of blankets, Foster tapped the back of the wagon's headboard. "We're ready, Reese."

The elderly chauffeur turned and winked at Marina. "Evening, Mrs. Delaney."

She beamed with pleasure, loving the way it sounded to be addressed as Mrs. Delaney. "Good evening, Reese."

As the wagon lurched forward, Foster gathered her into his arms. "So how *does* autumn feel in my arms, anyway?"

Pondering a future in which *all* the seasons of her life would be filled with moments like this one, Marina shook her head, overwhelmed. "I can't seem to find the words—"

"Sweetheart," he murmured against her lips, "you won't need them tonight."

About the Author

Sherene Funk is a voracious reader and hopeless romantic who owns more books than she can ever read in this lifetime—but that doesn't stop her from collecting more. A graduate from Brigham Young University in 1992 with a degree in American studies, she worked in advertising and marketing before moving on to website content writing.

She has published several humorous nonfiction articles in her local newspaper, including "My New Year's Opportunity," "Clumsy Moments, Laughs for Years," "Next Year Anniversary Inn," and "One Woman's Alaskan Fish Tale," but she much prefers writing pure escapism and stories about happily ever after.

Sherene is currently living her own fairy tale romance in Spanish Fork, Utah, with her husband of over twenty-one years.

Autumn in Your Arms is her first novel but hopefully not her last.

70505867R00106

Made in the USA
San Bernardino, CA
02 March 2018